# THE HOLE

William Meikle

First Edition
ISBN 978-1-937771-97-3



A DarkFuse Release
www.darkfuse.com

Join the Newsletter:
http://eepurl.com/jOH5

Become a fan on Facebook:
www.facebook.com/darkfuse

Follow us on Twitter:
www.twitter.com/darkfuse

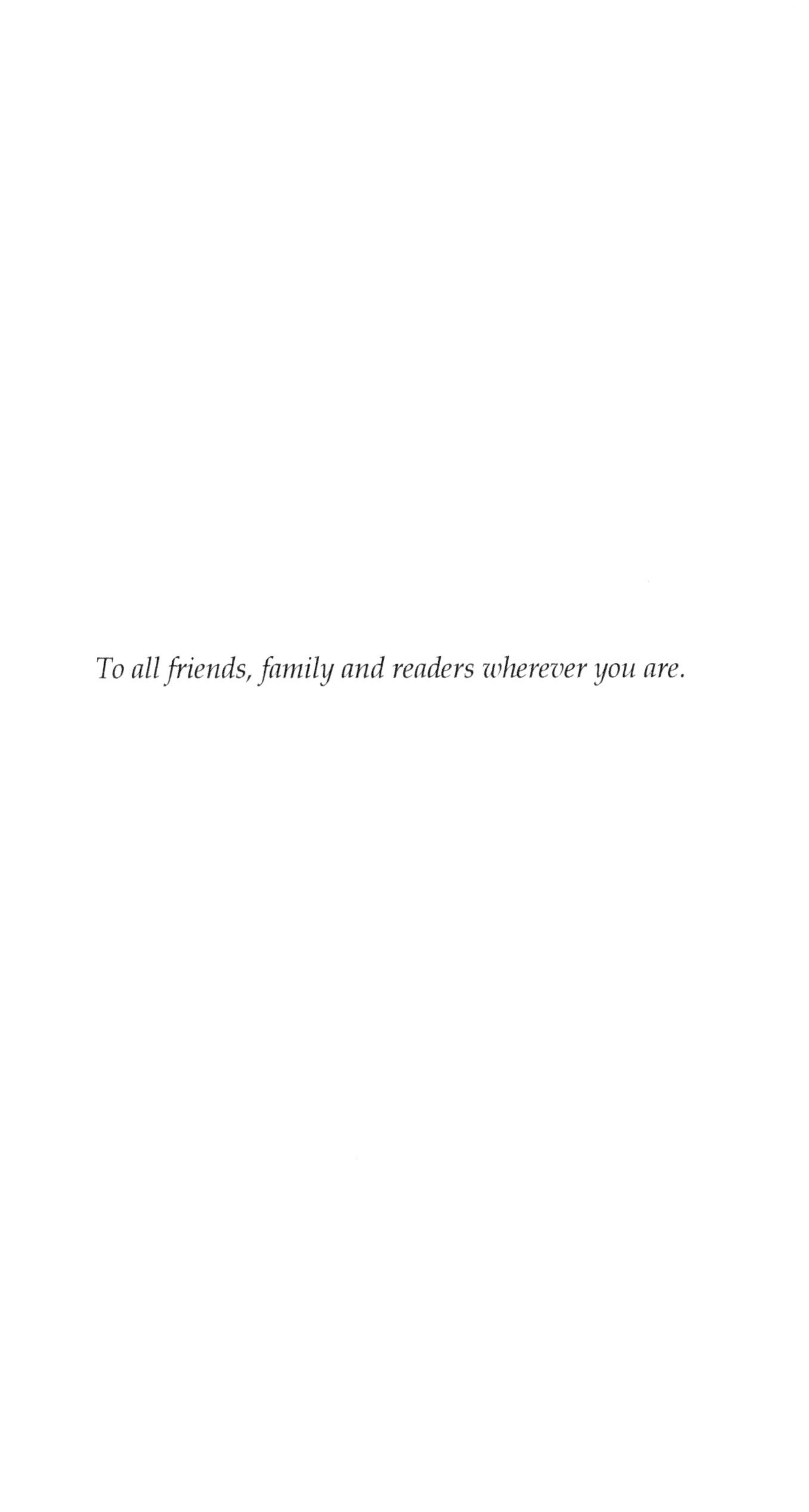

*To all friends, family and readers wherever you are.*

**Acknowledgements**

Thanks to everybody at DarkFuse for all the effort that goes into the books that no one ever sees. It's much appreciated.

# 1

The hum started just after midnight.

The first person to notice was Fred Grant. He heard it initially just as he left The Roadside, and to start with he just put it down to a particularly heavy truck somewhere nearby on the highway; a low drone, distant but slowly getting louder. He paid it no mind, for truck noise in itself wasn't unusual in these parts. The highway was a through route to larger towns and cities to the south, and the bar was a popular stopping spot for trucks from all over the East Coast, at least during the hours it was open.

Fred took a piss in the parking lot while giving the booze time to see if he was able to walk, having to do a little drunken dance to maintain his balance, then another to avoid squirting himself in the pants leg. He stuck a smoke in the corner of his mouth, got it lit on the third attempt, and headed off in the general direction of home.

The hum persisted, and seemed to keep pace with him as he made his way through town. He noticed it, vaguely, like a bee buzzing nearby on a summer day, but he'd had too much beer to consider its persistence strange. His mind, what little of it that was still active after the booze, was more concerned with walking in a straight line and reaching his bed before he collapsed.

The town was quiet...the town was almost always quiet. True, the area around the trailer park could get boisterous in summer during barbecue and beer season, but now that winter was approaching folks tended to stay indoors when dark fell and the temperature took a tumble. There wasn't any frost on the ground yet, but it surely wasn't far off. But indoors, at least in his place, wasn't anywhere that Fred wanted to be. Too much time alone meant too much thinking, and that just led to trouble. At least among other folks he could lose himself for a while, and shut down the clamor in his head.

He hadn't gone out with the intention of getting wasted, but one beer had led to another. Then a winning run on the pool table netted him a hundred bucks to blow on hard liquor and after a few JDs nothing much seemed to matter beyond getting more inside him. He had a vague memory of Tony telling him he'd had enough, and being too drunk to argue. The hit of fresh air on top of the booze guaranteed that oblivion wasn't going to be too far off. He should have felt remorse, even shame at the state he'd got himself into, but lately his give-a-fuck meter had been broken, and he wasn't planning to get it fixed anytime soon.

The hum was still there as he walked round the side of his trailer, and when he stumbled and almost fell trying to get his key from his trouser pocket, the walls vibrated noticeably under the hand he put out to steady himself. The booze haze lifted enough to lend him the merest twitch of curiosity; just enough to make him stand still and listen.

It sounded less like a truck now, more like heavy machinery, the hum mixed with a grinding vibration that he felt through his shoes and in his jaw, where it threatened to rattle his teeth. It came from nowhere and everywhere. He turned full circle but could not pinpoint any obvious directionality; there was no indication of a source. And he wasn't curious enough to wander off looking for one.

He got the key in the lock on the third attempt, almost fell up the first step, and hauled himself into the trailer. As he headed for the bottle of rye in the kitchen he felt the hum again, throbbing just underfoot, but when he fell into his chair and turned on the television, the vibration dwindled and faded into the background.

He promptly forgot all about it as he topped his booze level back up to maximum.

*I drink to forget. Forget what? I don't remember.*

But the trouble was, he did remember, and whatever booze he'd got inside him tonight, it still wasn't enough. When he closed his eyes, he saw the accident replaying again; the headlights picking out the deer, the slow-motion panic as he realized he couldn't swerve far enough to miss it. He could still hear the sickening thud as the animal suddenly disappeared from view and the trees rushed forward to meet the car, too fast to avoid. Once again he heard the crunch of metal and felt glass on his arms and in his face as the windscreen shattered and fell on him. He tried to get out of the vehicle, tried to flee the scene, but he was trapped in the seat, stuck there until they found him. Again. He had a record. Again. And he lost his job. Again.

He sat in the chair, staring at the television without a clue as to what he was watching, smoking a succession of cigarettes and chugging more whiskey. And finally, he'd had enough. The empty bottle fell to the floor, and Fred fell into a stupor.

In the morning he woke up, groaned, and dragged his hangover to the washroom. Small furry animals had slept in his mouth, his guts roiled, and a small man with a jackhammer had taken up residence behind his right eye. He stood over the urinal, concentrating on not throwing up.

*The things we do for love.*

Something red at the corner of his eye caught his attention and he turned, looking at his reflection in the mirror above the sink. At first he couldn't make sense of what he was looking at, his addled brain struggling to process the facts. He put a hand up, tentatively, and prodded the red area where it was at its most intense, at his nose and lips. His fingers touched sticky, coagulated blood.

He'd suffered a nosebleed in the night; so severe that his shirt was soaked red from neck to belt.

# 2

Janet Dickson barely had time to open the door in the morning before the office space she rather grandly called *The Surgery* started to fill up. Most mornings she'd see one or two walk-in patients this early, and then have time for a leisurely coffee and a bagel before starting her scheduled appointments at ten.

Normally she'd see a maximum of twenty patients a day, but twice that number had already filed into the waiting room, and more cars were arriving outside every minute. It was already obvious that her schedule for the day was no more than a forlorn hope, and that she had to steel herself for not only dealing with the walk-ins, but also explaining to those who already had appointments that she wouldn't be able to honor the agreement.

*I need a receptionist.*

She laughed at the thought. She barely made enough money to pay her own bills. The town just wasn't big enough to warrant hiring more staff. It was normally too quiet. That was why she'd come here. A year in a big-city hospital dealing with every ailment modern civilization could throw at her had burned out most of her idealism, but she still thought she could make a difference, somewhere quieter... somewhere slower. She had thought she'd chosen the perfect town, with a low crime rate, healthy outdoor lifestyles, and just enough elderly and children to keep her busy. Most of the time she had a relaxed and stress-free day.

*Except for today.*

"Try to form a queue," she shouted above the hubbub. "I'll get to you all eventually. And if anybody wants to go for a coffee, I'll have a large latte."

That got her a laugh and at least broke some of the tension in the room. But it was obvious that something had the townsfolk spooked.

She heard about *the hum* from her second patient. On a normal visiting day Ellen Simmons would have been first in line, first with the gossip, and usually with a different complaint from the one she'd protested long and loud about on her last visit. Today the older woman had to play second fiddle to Jim McClay, and she was none too happy about having to wait the extra two minutes.

"There's nothing wrong with that man that a hard day's work wouldn't cure," was the first thing she said as she closed the door behind her.

"That's your medical opinion, is it, Ellen?" Janet said, trying, but not completely succeeding, to keep exasperation out of her voice.

"Don't need no medical opinion to know a slacker when I see one. You're a soft touch, Doc. And everybody knows it. Why, just yesterday, Mrs. Ellinson said..."

And that was the start of a litany of perceived slights and scurrilous gossip that Janet had learned a long time ago was best ignored. She only started to pay attention when the woman mentioned waking up in the night.

"It was terrible. At first I thought it was an earthquake. The whole room shook, and two of my best china figures fell off the dressing table. I'm not even sure glue will fix them. I had them off my Frank's mother for our first anniversary. Did I ever tell you..."

Janet gave the woman a verbal prod, otherwise the story she actually wanted to hear might never get told, lost in a labyrinthine pathway of Ellen Simmons' stray thoughts made verbal.

"What time was this?" Janet asked.

The older woman looked none too pleased to be interrupted, but gave in when Janet raised an eyebrow.

"Around one," she finally said. "And it got worse right quick soon after. I thought my head was going to explode. Like having a dentist drilling into my skull. Then the nosebleed came...all over my best nightgown and down across the quilt. I'll never get the stain out. I said to Mrs. Hewitt out in the waiting room, 'Who's going to pay, that's what I want to know?' and do you know what that bitch said?"

Janet tuned the woman out again. Ellen Simmons was in her early fifties, but she had the dress code and mannerisms of someone twenty years older. She reminded Janet of one of her own aunts, a widow from the age of twenty who reached eighty-five without having a good word to say about anybody, her face as dry and sour as her heart. Ellen had tried over the past few months to get Janet involved in what she called *the life of the town*—needlework classes, baking classes, Bible readings. Each time Janet had refused, politely but firmly, and each time Ellen Simmons got a little colder and a little more cutting in her tone. Janet guessed that she might be the subject of some gossip on her own behalf outside the surgery.

*But that's where it is, outside the surgery. It's of little importance.*

She'd lost the train of the conversation in her reverie; her hands had been working in a routine of dabbing and cleaning while the older woman talked. It was obvious that Ellen Simmons was waiting for an answer to a question Janet hadn't heard. She made a noncommittal *'um,'* hoping that was enough to satisfy the woman. It seemed to do the trick. Ellen Simmons left, but as ever, she had a passing barb to fling.

"It'll be something to do with that damned trailer park. You mark my words."

The morning got steadily busier, mostly nosebleeds and headaches of varying degrees of severity. She sent some of them next door to the pharmacy for pills and cotton swabs, but others needed closer attention, particularly the elderly and the young. Two in particular gave cause for concern; old man Parks was white, his eyes fluttering and pulse racing, while young Joshua Timmons bled both nasally and rectally. By the time Janet got an ambulance organized and got them headed at speed up the road to County, she had thirty more people stuffed into her small waiting room and spilling out into the parking bay outside.

Over the course of a manic morning she was to hear many more tales of splitting headaches and nosebleeds, strange vibrations and worries of earthquakes. She didn't see the pattern until she got a break at lunchtime, and by then the source was all too obvious.

# 3

Fred had been up for the best part of an hour. The nosebleed had obviously stopped of its own accord overnight, but he stood at the washroom mirror for a long time before he could bring himself to clean up the mess. He was frightened that if he touched the coagulated blob below his nostril and dislodged it, he might let loose a flow he couldn't stop.

*Is this it? Is this the first sign?*

He'd been drinking constantly for months now. Tony at the bar had warned it was all going to catch up to him one of these days. But *one of these days* hadn't come, and Fred had kept at the booze like a man on a mission.

*And now here it is.*

He found that it actually worried him. Not enough to get him to stop, but enough for him to think that he might do so…sometime. That thought was enough to get him moving. He dabbed at his nose, gingerly at first, then with more intent when he saw he was in no imminent danger of bleeding out. He was relieved to find that he cleaned up nicely, the blood washing off and leaving no trace behind apart from a still-raw tenderness in each nostril and a taste of copper at the back of his throat.

*If only everything could be wiped so readily.*

He had finished his third smoke and had just fetched the first beer of the day from the fridge when someone knocked on the trailer door. He ignored it to start with, and turned up the television, but the knocking got more insistent. Whoever was there knew Fred was inside, and wasn't about to take no for an answer.

"Come on, lad, get your shit together," a well-known voice shouted. "I got a job for you. Cash in hand, no questions asked."

Fred knew Charlie Watson's kind of jobs. Shit shoveling, garbage collecting, septic tank cleaning—all the crap nobody else wanted to deal with.

*Except those that don't have any other choice. Those like me.*

Charlie knocked again.

"Fuck off. I'm not here," Fred shouted.

He heard the old man laugh.

"A hundred bucks says you are."

A hundred bucks would cover his booze bill for the coming weekend. That got him out of his chair. He rose and put the beer back in the fridge.

"Later, baby," he whispered, and opened the trailer door.

Charlie spat out a thick clump of tobacco and squinted up at Fred.

"You look like warmed-up shit, boy," the older man said. "You need to cut down on the booze."

"You're one to talk," Fred replied, and lit up another smoke, making sure he kept upwind of Charlie. Some days the stench was enough to make you gag. It wasn't so bad this morning, but the odd-job man still smelled like a wet dog that had rolled in a cow pat, and he looked like he'd been soaking in shit and piss his whole life—which wasn't too far off the mark these past few years. Charlie was Fred's main drinking buddy, a man who could be relied on for company at any bar in town, and a willing ally in the quest for oblivion after a bad day. When he wasn't doing that, he was trying to find enough dirty work to pay for his nights. It looked like he'd found something.

"So what's the job?" Fred asked. He spotted that Charlie had a red stain in his moustache, to match the yellow nicotine streak in the gray. He remembered his own nosebleed, and the futile efforts to clean a shirt that was now consigned to the garbage bag.

"Something's going on in Hopman's Hollow," Charlie replied, heading for his battered pickup, expecting Fred to follow. "Ain't too sure what yet, just that there's a shitload of clearing up to do, and the money's there, if you want it?"

"I want it," Fred called after him. "Give me a second."

He went back inside the trailer and changed into his work gear—a denim shirt and Wranglers that might last out the year if he didn't put too much effort in. His work boots were in a similar state of disrepair, the left one starting to come away from the sole.

*But beggars can't be choosers.*

He pulled the boots on, only then realizing that they were still damp from three days before when Charlie had them clearing out a creek on the west side of town. He squelched slightly as he stepped down out of the trailer.

Charlie was already in the pickup, waiting, a crumpled smoke dangling from the right side of his mouth. Fred got in the passenger seat, sat as close to the door as he could, and rolled down the window. If anything, the smell was worse inside the truck, and even lighting a cigarette of his own didn't help matters. He breathed through his mouth. It helped some, but not much. He was grateful he hadn't managed to eat any breakfast, for it would surely have made another appearance by now.

The old man didn't seem to notice. He put the truck in gear, an action that made the old box creak and grind. The muffler let out two loud bangs, and the truck finally wheezed into life and crept away from the trailer. The vehicle didn't have many more miles left in it.

*Much like me*, Fred thought, then smacked himself on the forehead with the palm of his hand. He was spending too much time locked in his head. Maybe this jaunt with Charlie was just what was needed to take his mind off things.

If Charlie saw Fred's frustration, he didn't mention it.

"Some news, huh?" the old man said as they drove through the trailer park.

"Ain't seen any yet," Fred replied, intent on keeping any chat to a minimum until he could get out into the fresh air. "What's up?"

"Just half the town coming down sick, that's what's up," Charlie replied, and laughed, a high whiny thing like a hyena in pain. "Headaches and nosebleeds. Even had a touch of it myself just after midnight, but a couple of slugs of Jack put paid to it quick enough. Ain't a headache in the world that Jack can't shift."

"Amen to that," Fred replied, and wished, not for the last time that morning, that he'd stayed in his trailer and tested that hypothesis.

* * *

Fall was almost over. The trees lining the highway had lost the vibrant red and oranges from their foliage and had settled for dirty brown scraps that fluttered and fell like dying birds in the slight breeze. The sky hung over them like a piece of blue porcelain, and the wind coming through the open window was bracing, to say the least. But as the old truck gained speed, Charlie's body odor seemed to dispel, and Fred even started to enjoy the ride.

Unfortunately, they weren't going far.

*Not nearly far enough.*

Hopman's Hollow was little more than a boggy pond a mile out on the eastern edge of town, just off the main highway. Or rather, it had been when Fred last passed it a week before. Since then it had taken on pretensions of being a small lake, having grown to three times its previous size. It now covered an area nearly the size of a football field, and the murky water lapped up close to the road.

As they got closer still, Fred saw that a small off-shoot from the main body of water had undermined a patch of John Hopman's land at the rear of his house. Fred's heart sank as he saw the exposed septic tank, its contents clearly oozing from a rupture at the rear end into the new expanse of pond below it. The tank itself, a cylinder some eight feet long and four feet in diameter, hung precariously over the new shoreline.

*More shit shoveling.*

John Hopman stood on his lawn, arms crossed, staring grimly at the enlarged hollow. He acknowledged their presence with a nod as they parked at the end of his drive.

"Think you can do something, Charlie?" the landowner said.

The landowner had a drop of fresh blood under his left nostril, but Fred knew better than to mention it. There was little sense in further riling a man who was clearly in a foul mood. Besides, the Hopmans weren't known for their goodwill and hospitality. The family had been the richest folks in town for over a century now; most land, biggest house, and loudest voice in any decisions made by the town council. They were feared and hated in equal measure, but never loved, and Fred had always tried to keep his dealings with them to a minimum. He was surprised that Charlie had brought them here in the first place, for the old man had, on many occasions, made his feelings about *the first family* perfectly clear.

*Parasites, leeches and worms; and that's just the good ones.*

Fred was woolgathering. Again. He nodded in John Hopman's direction, and turned to go after

Charlie.

The older man was already over by the septic tank. Fred walked over to join him, aware that the *hum* was back—distant but noticeable. His headache returned with a vengeance, pounding behind his right eye.

"Get over here, lad," Charlie said. "It's going to take both of us to stop this booger toppling over. Ain't like it's the first time I've had you work through a hangover, is it?"

Seconds later Fred was knee deep in muddy water that had too many suspicious bits floating in it to think about. He had most of the weight of the septic tank on his shoulder, and as Charlie pushed from one side some of the contents spilled out and ran down the front of Fred's shirt.

*Another one ruined.*

Fred took as much of the weight as he could, and tried not to breathe too heavily as Charlie attempted to right the tank. From what Fred could see, it wasn't going to happen—they'd need some heavy lifting gear to help. He was about to tell that to Charlie when things got a lot worse.

It happened fast.

Hopman was being sensible and stood well back, which was just as well for the bank that had been supporting the tank gave way completely, sending it, and the two workmen, tumbling into deeper water. The edge of the tank struck Charlie a glancing blow on the brow. Fred saw blood spurt, just before the older man and the tank started to sink. As he started to go under, Charlie's eyes rolled up to show only white.

Fred didn't wait to think. He let go of the tank and dived for Charlie, catching the man just as his head dipped below the surface. He was aware that the septic tank was sinking fast, burps and gurgles accompanying it as it fell from sight, but Fred was fixed on helping the older man. He gathered Charlie up in his arms and, making sure he had solid footing beneath him, started to wade back toward the new area of banking. He was dismayed to see the sides crumble away from him, the pond growing faster than his wading pace. Hopman was still up on his rapidly shrinking lawn, staring aghast at the growing expanse of muddy water that threatened to overwhelm his property.

"Give me a hand here," Fred shouted. At the same moment he felt the water *sucking* at his legs, threatening to sweep him off his feet. He struggled forward as fast as he could manage, Charlie a dead weight in his arms.

Hopman's gaze shifted, looking over Fred's shoulder. The landowner's face went white, and Fred didn't have to look back to know he was in trouble. The tugging at his legs got stronger fast and seconds later the current lifted his feet off the bottom. He rearranged his hold on Charlie to ensure the man's mouth would stay above water and started to swim with his free arm, kicking hard. The tide pulled harder.

"For pity's sake, Hopman, help us," he shouted.

The man didn't move, his gaze fixed on the center of the pond, eyes wide; mouth open in astonishment.

Fred put all he had into the swimming stroke. He finally felt something solid underneath him and was able to plant his legs down. It had to be the septic tank, lodged somewhere below on the bed of the pond. He stumbled and fell forward, just as the water sucked away from beneath him, as if someone had pulled out a plug. The tide pulled at Charlie, threatened to tug him out of Fred's grasp. He gripped tightly at the old man's shirt, praying that it would hold. Water roared and foamed all around him.

Suddenly all went quiet.

Fred, with Charlie beside him, lay across the top of the septic tank, half of which was embedded in a steep muddy bank.

* * *

A voice called down to them.

"You still alive down there?"

John Hopman was some feet above, looking down, then past them. Fred followed his gaze and almost forgot to breathe.

The septic tank was perched on the edge of a drop that fell away out of his view, but the sound of water dropping into the new chasm told him it was of some depth. The pond no longer existed. In its place was a huge muddy hole that even now was falling in at the edges, soft clay soil seeping farther into the gaping hole.

Fred shifted his weight, and the septic tank lurched to one side alarmingly before settling again.

"Get some rope," he said to Hopman. "And you'd better do it quick."

Hopman complied this time, and moved away out of sight. Fred made sure that they were in no immediate danger of toppling backward into the hole, and checked on Charlie. The older man was out cold, his face white with only a high patch of color on each cheek. The wound at his brow looked superficial, although it was still bleeding, and he was breathing, fast and shallow, but breathing.

"Stay with me, Charlie," Fred whispered. "You're the only friend I've got in this town."

Hopman came back seconds later.

"Grab hold," he shouted, and threw down, not a rope, but a long length of exterior electric cabling. Fred had to shift his footing to get it wrapped under Charlie's armpits, and his heart thudded faster as the septic tank slid back a foot before coming to a stop. He tied the cable in a knot he prayed was strong enough to hold.

"Okay, take him up," he shouted. He hoisted Charlie's weight as long as he could while Hopman took the strain. As Hopman started to haul Charlie up, Fred stepped off the tank and tried to climb the bank to keep pace. There was a crash behind him. He turned in time to see the septic tank fall away out of sight. The thud as it hit bottom seemed to take a long time to come.

Then Fred was in a scramble for his life as the soil sloughed away beneath his hands and feet. He slid back three feet before he caught purchase, his legs swinging over empty air.

He looked down.

The hole fell away into a dark pit far below. Something moved down there, something large and pale, but it was gone before he could make out what it was. He grabbed at a thick root, half expecting it to give way beneath his weight. But to his surprise and relief it held, long enough for him to clamber away from the lip of the hole and roll aside; traversing the rest of the muddy bank in a zigzag crawl that brought him within range of Hopman's reaching hand.

He took it gratefully, and let the man pull him up onto the lawn where he lay beside Charlie's unconscious body, gasping in air, wondering what had just happened, and wiping away a fresh nosebleed.

# 4

Janet Dickson had just realized that all of her patients that morning were from the east side of town. She decided that the sheriff needed to know, and was reaching for the phone when Fred Grant arrived in the waiting room, half carrying Charlie Watson. The older man had blood seeping from a scalp wound and looked to be unsteady on his feet. She put the phone down and moved quickly to help. She couldn't miss noticing the rank smell that hung around the men, but ignored it as she helped Fred get Charlie to the treatment room.

"I'm fine," the wounded man said and tried to push them away. "Ain't nothing a little Jack won't cure."

"I'll be the judge of that," Janet said. She finally persuaded the older man to sit on one of the gurneys, and set about trying to clean the wound.

"It's a nasty cut. What happened to you?" she asked.

It was Fred who replied.

"John Hopman's septic tank fell on him," he said, deadpan.

Janet almost laughed but stopped when she saw he was serious. And she was now also intrigued, so she let Fred stay while she stitched Charlie up, the story unfolding as she did so. "It's a big hole?" she asked as both the story and the stitching came to a conclusion.

Fred nodded.

"And getting bigger by the looks of things. I wouldn't be surprised if the Hopman house isn't at risk before the day is out."

"Any idea what's caused it?"

"Nope," Fred replied. "But I'll tell you something—ain't no way I'll be the one cleaning that shit up."

The youth was more talkative than she'd ever seen him. He wasn't one of her patients, but she knew of him, of course. Everybody knew the town *bad boy*.

"Twenty years old and fit for nothing but the county jail," was how Sheriff Bill Wozniak described him. Janet didn't quite see it that way. She liked the youth. He had a good head on his shoulders. He and Charlie had painted the outside of her house just after she moved in, and it was obvious that both men took some pride in doing the job properly. Fred hadn't come across as brash or mouthy like others of his generation.

Of course just last year he'd smashed up a car he'd stolen mere hours before. But he'd admitted it straightaway the next morning, and had even appeared contrite, blaming it on the booze and promising to behave in the future. Whether he could deliver on that promise remained to be seen. But here and now in the surgery he looked like what he was—an excited youth running on adrenaline and fumes.

There was one other thing. Both men had nosebleeds that took a long time to stop flowing. Charlie had more blood coming from his nose than from the scalp wound.

"Headache?" Janet asked.

Fred smiled wanly. "No, thanks. I've already got one. And it's a real stinker. It got worse right after we arrived at Hopman's place and it ain't eased much since."

That statement set alarm bells ringing in Janet's mind. After she showed the two men out with prescriptions for painkillers, and a warning to stay off the booze and take it easy, she went to the wall map and traced her finger over the houses of the patients who seemed worst afflicted. She'd been right in her earlier assumption. All of the cases came from the east side of town, the worst being those closest to Hopman's Hollow.

Her patients' ailments, and the new hole, were linked.

*But for the life of me I can't see how.*

* * *

She was still pondering the question later that afternoon when Bill Wozniak arrived. By then the nosebleeds and headaches had all been seen to, and she'd checked with County that the two patients she'd sent over were fine. For the first time since her arrival that morning there were no patients in the waiting room and no appointments scheduled. She felt safe in making herself a coffee, and had just sat back at her desk when the sheriff arrived. The big man looked worried.

"You look like you need a coffee," she said.

He shook his head, and she knew there was trouble. Anything that kept the big man from his fix could be nothing less. He looked older than his forty-four years, and seemed somehow slumped, as if suddenly beset by the strain of his office, a strain he had always seemed to carry lightly until now.

"It ain't good, Janet," he said. "It ain't good at all. I need you to come with me to the Hopman place. We've got a forensic team coming down from County, but it'll be a while yet before they're here, and it'll be getting dark. Maybe you'll see something in daylight before then that'll give me a heads up on what is going on."

"What *is* going on?" she asked.

"I ain't exactly sure myself, yet. I have my suspicions. But I'd rather let you make up your own mind. Will you come?"

"Of course, just give me five minutes to close up."

* * *

It was obvious before they even reached the Hopman place that something was indeed going on. There was more traffic on the road than she had ever seen. Normally you could drive along this stretch and maybe see a lorry going the other way, or a battered pickup heading for one of the farms. Now it seemed that half the town was heading out east. Whatever it was, it had brought out as many people as the church summer fete.

Bill had been remarkably quiet on the short trip from the town center, but now he cursed, long and loud.

"Ain't had a day like this since '98 when the school bus crashed," he said. He waved a hand to encompass the traffic. "Damned ambulance chasers. I'd have the lot of them in the cells if I had the room."

"*Ambulance chasers?* I thought it was only Charlie who got hurt?"

"Hurt? There's more than hurt out here, Janet," Bill said softly. "We got some dead folks."

He went pale, and there was something in his eyes that made Janet wish she'd stayed back in the surgery.

*It's a bad one.*

She didn't push it, for by then they were almost on top of a crowd of gawkers. They were packed so thick on the roadside that Bill had to put on his lights and siren and edge his way through, window down, shouting curses and exhortations at the top of his voice. Even then they scarcely moved—not until Bill started to *accidentally* nudge them aside with the front bumpers.

It was only when they got through the crowd that Janet finally saw what all the fuss was about. The Hopman house, or rather half of it, sat perched on the edge of a hole that stretched off quarter of a mile to the south. What was left of the building was open to the elements, the rest obviously having fallen away when the ground collapsed beneath it. There was a fine array of antique furniture on show to the world. Janet knew that as much again and more must have joined the walls in their fall into the hole. If nothing else, the Hopmans had already lost a small fortune.

At the nearest point to their position the collapse reached all the way up to the edge of the road, where a quartet of tired-looking deputies tried to keep the crowd back. The scar was also over a hundred yards wide, and as deep as Fred Grant had said, if not deeper, a yawning chasm filled with blackness.

"It's still growing," Bill said quietly, as he got out of the car.

Janet got out and joined him.

As if to prove Bill's point, a foot-wide piece of the right-hand roadway fell off into the hole and tumbled away out of sight. She waited for a splash, but none came, or if it did, it was too far off to hear. People started to crowd closer, hoping for a better look.

"Get these folks right back," Bill shouted. "And get this road closed. I want roadblocks a hundred yards either side of the collapsed area. There's to be no traffic either way until I say so."

The deputies moved to comply. Bill turned to Janet.

"This isn't why you're here. Come with me."

He led her west along the road, back towards town, then along the side of the hole for fifty yards. Her heart sank when she saw the bodies, three of them, lying on the edge on a bed of pine needles. From a distance it looked to be two adults and a child. They were unclothed, with the greasy pallor of flesh that had been too long in the water.

*Floaters.*

She steeled herself for the inevitable stench to come. As she approached, she noticed something else.

*They scarcely look human.*

"What is this, Bill? An accident?"

"You tell me, Doc," the sheriff said wearily. "I only work here."

He looked green around the gills, as if about to puke. She saw why as she got closer. All three bodies were bloated and distended, puffed up by gasses. The degree of decomposition seemed severe.

*And it'll only get worse out here.*

"We need to get these into controlled conditions, fast," Janet said. "Otherwise there won't be much left for the boys from County to examine."

"That might be for the best," Bill said dryly, but didn't elaborate.

He stayed well back as Janet bent to look at the bodies. The decomposition was indeed bad, and getting rapidly worse, as if the air itself was acting like acid on the pale flesh. The incongruities piled up as soon as she started her examination. The first thing that struck her was that all three bodies seemed to be completely hairless. Then she saw the tails...three feet long, gray and scaly, the sort of thing normally seen on rats. The more she looked the more she saw that these bodies were indeed not human. They *were* mammalian, of sorts, but looked to have evolved for a different existence. For eyes they only had black pits, their hands were flat and broad, palms like spades, fingers stubby, and their back legs were thick and short, built for pushing rather than walking.

She looked up at Bill, who was pointedly looking anywhere but at the bodies.

"What the hell is this?" she said. "Some kind of joke?"

Bill looked solemn.

"*Hell* might be the operative word," he said, and pointed at the head of one of the bodies. Twin protuberances, fleshy and swollen poked from above the brow. "Sure looks like horns to me."

It took Janet a few seconds to understand.

"Devils? You think that's what these are?"

Bill shrugged. "If the shoe fits..."

She almost laughed, and then thought better of it. Bill was a churchman through and through, as was much of the town. She'd learned a long time ago to keep any skepticism to herself. She did, however, study the horns more closely. There was no sign of any bone. Instead the bumps seemed to be coated with short fine hairs, and she guessed they might be some kind of sensory organs. She bent to study the mouth area when the face of the thing fell in with a moist sucking sound, and she almost gagged as a foul stench rose up from the body, forcing her to cover her mouth. The chest cavity started to slump in on itself, and the smell got much worse.

It quickly became clear she wasn't going to get much, if anything, of the remains back to controlled conditions. They were corroding fast, noxious fluids bubbling and seeping into the ground as Janet watched. There wasn't even any hope of bones to study—the whole structure of the bodies was breaking down and in seconds there was nothing left but some greasy flesh on the pine needles.

She just had time to scrape a sample of what remained into one of her latex gloves before, with a soft hiss, the last of it turned to little more than a puff of steam.

"You can cancel the forensics team," she said.

* * *

She stood back from where the bodies had lain and started to study the surrounding ground. Bill pulled her away, grabbing her arm hard enough that she knew there would be a bruise there later.

"What the hell did you do that for?"

Then she heard it, a hum, like the sound of distant machinery. She tasted blood on her lip from a nosebleed, and a headache pounded behind her left eye.

"It's happening again," the sheriff said, and pointed at the hole. The sides were slipping, falling away into the blackness, and the crumbling edge crept towards their feet.

"Come on," Bill said. "Back to the car."

They almost didn't make it. The side of the hole collapsed faster than their walking pace. Janet stumbled, right on the edge, as a fresh chunk of earth fell away underfoot, and was only saved by Bill bodily lifting her up and away to safety. Seconds later they were both running, just ahead of collapsing soil and rock. A tree crashed to ground right behind them, then another.

They got halfway to the road when the screaming started, and when they reached the tarmac, they had to push through a panicked throng, all trying to flee in the opposite direction.

"Get behind me," Bill said, and using his bulk, pushed back against the crowd, utilizing his huge arms to shove anyone aside who was foolish enough to get close.

"Coming through," he shouted, and enough folk moved aside that they were finally able to get to the squad car. Over to their left the hole had encroached on the road itself. A hefty slab of hardtop fell away less than twelve feet away as they got into the vehicle.

"Time to go," Bill said grimly, shoved the car into reverse and screeched away as the whole road fell in just beyond the bonnet in a crash of noise and a billow of dust. Janet smelt burning rubber as the tires squealed, then held their grip. The car shot backwards, away from an approaching collapse.

"Get out the goddamned way," Bill shouted, then had to brake hard as they caught up with the fleeing crowd. For a long moment Janet thought they had not gone far enough; the road continued to collapse as the hole widened farther. She held her breath as a fresh plume of dusty earth flew up just in front of them.

Bill killed the engine. There was no road to be seen beyond the bonnet, just a black hole full of swirling dust.

After a few seconds Janet remembered to breathe. The collapse seemed to be over…for now.

Everything went quiet.

# 5

Fred and Charlie sat at the bar in The Roadside, on their second beer, working on making it a third before too long, when news came in that The Hollow had grown again. The news was brought by Tom Perkins, as red as a berry and excited fit to bust.

"The Hopman place has gone; most of the house, stables, horses and paddock, the whole lot, all 'et up. And the highway's out; ain't nothing coming in from that direction for a long time. You gotta come see."

The bar fell quiet as many of the clientele left to check it out, but Fred and Charlie stayed in their seats.

"Ain't you boys going to see what all the fuss is about?" Tony, the barkeep, asked.

"It's a big hole, I've seen more than enough of it already," Fred said, finishing off his beer. Charlie merely grunted, and chugged his own glass down. His scalp wound was red raw, black stitches showing under butterfly clip bandages that already looked grimy. The wound hadn't slowed down his beer drinking any though, and Fred was happy to go along with a third for each of them. When he reached for his wallet, Charlie waved him away.

"The beers are on me tonight, son. I owe you, for getting me out of that hole."

Fred wasn't about to argue. There didn't look like any way they'd get paid by John Hopman anytime soon, and he was going to need most of whatever cash he had in his pocket for food for the next week. But although they were only on the third beer, Fred could already hear the JD calling. He suspected eating would just have to wait. But before then, he needed to slow down a tad; it was too early in the day to start tying one on.

*Who am I kidding?*

"What do you think is causing it?" he asked Charlie, hoping to get a conversation going that might take his mind off the booze, for a few seconds at least.

Charlie accepted his fresh beer and chugged down a third of it before replying.

"If I was betting on it, my money would be on the old mine workings. It was only a matter of time before a collapse happened. Looks like that time has come."

Fred knew of the mines; every kid in town knew. Back in junior high, one of the top dares of a summer was to go inside the main entrance at the foot of Hangman's Bluff and stay there after sundown. Fred remembered his own experience only too well. A cold evening in a damp place; the only scares being ones he gave to himself and a slap from the old man on his late return home. Not much reward for surviving a successful dare. But he hadn't gone much farther than a couple of yards inside. He might have been stupid enough to accept the dare—but he wasn't *that* stupid.

All he remembered of it now was the dark and the damp. Even back then in the early years of the new century, the place had looked to be long neglected.

"I never knew that the mine had ever amounted to much," he said. "Didn't old man Hopman give up on it back in the sixties?"

Charlie took a while to answer, and when he did, he had a look around first to make sure no one else was listening.

"That was the story he had put around. But some of us know better."

Fred lit up a smoke and sipped at his beer. He knew Charlie of old. A story was coming, and one that might be a while in the telling.

* * *

"You've got to remember," Charlie started. "Things was different back in them days. There weren't none of these Health and Safety restrictions...at least none that old man Hopman needed to pay much attention to in any case. I weren't much older than you are now, fresh back from 'Nam with a busted knee and not enough dollars to keep me in booze and smokes. When word came down that the old man was hiring miners, cash in hand, no questions asked, I jumped at the chance.

"Mayhap I should've been more careful, but the

money was too good to turn down. Hopman even provided us with free meals and as much coffee as we could drink after our shift was done. But the working conditions in the shaft itself were a bad dream come true. He had six of us down there, three at a time in twelve-hour shifts, hacking away in the near dark with scarcely a pit prop or lintel to stop the rock from falling in on us.

"I don't mind telling you, there were a couple of times when things got right hairy. We nearly lost Tom Lipton when a stone fell on him. Banged his leg up good, and he was off work for a spell. But a couple of weeks later he was back at it with the rest of us. As I said already, the money was just too good to turn down.

"We never did find out what we were looking for. We shifted the rock and it was taken away in carts for the old man to inspect before it got dumped in the old quarry off the Getting's farm road. All we knew was that we had to keep digging. Old Hopman was on a quest for whatever it was he thought was down there. Silver was my thought, for there's stories from the old days of a vein running through the rock in these parts. But some of the men said it must be Spanish gold and others spoke of some long-forgotten stash of Indian treasure. There were even mutterings of it being a taboo place. Several local kids managed to scare themselves silly one night while partying a bit too hard. But this was at the ass end of the hippie era. There was more than just booze involved, if you catch my drift, and that waccy-baccy can make you see anything you want to see.

"In truth, nobody but old Hopman really knew, or

cared what we were digging for. We hacked at rock, coughed up dust, and took his money. We worked hard, and partied harder on the one day off we got in every ten. This was the early seventies, back when a party was a *real* party. This bar here was jumping most nights, and a man with a roll of green in his pocket was the most popular man in town. Happy days."

Charlie tailed off, staring into space, lost in memory. Fred thought the story was finished. But there was more to come.

"The good times lasted for six months," Charlie continued after a while. "Then one night the other shift disappeared. Nobody knows what happened, or when it happened. We turned up for our shift as usual in the morning to be faced, not with three tired men on the way out to meet us, but with a fresh cave-in. There was no blood, no sign at all the men had even been there except for a pickaxe and a shovel that had been bent out of shape, as if it had hit something, hard.

"We did what we could; we dug for three days straight, deep and far, only stopping for water and rest when we were too exhausted to keep going. We cleared the whole cave-in, and even dug a bit farther. But we never found nobody; no bodies, not a trace that they had ever been there."

Charlie stopped again and chugged what was left of his beer, motioning to Tony for another.

"Old man Hopman made a token effort to keep the work going, but ain't no way any of us was going back down there for a while, money or no money. And the old man himself seemed to have lost any enthusiasm he had for the project. I took up the handyman business, and tried to forget about the three men and what might have happened to them. I also took up the booze, even more than I had been doing. Some of them years are mighty cloudy looking back at them now. If you ain't careful, lad, you could be in for some of the same yourself."

Fred was in no mood for a lecture on abstinence.

*Not after the morning I had.*

"We're not talking about me," Fred interrupted. "Remember? There's more about the mines, isn't there?"

Charlie nodded.

"Just a bit. But give me time. I'm getting to it."

The older man lit a cigarette, taking his time about it, drawing out Fred's anticipation before finally continuing.

"I thought I was finished with the mine. But it weren't quite finished with me.

"It was nineteen eighty or thereabouts, eight years later, before I was back down there. Old man Hopman had got filthy rich at some point a few years before. I reckoned he'd finally found what he was looking for down there in the mine, but I'd scarcely given him any thought at all apart from in my nightmares—until the old man contracted me to get rid of some chemical waste from his factory over in Loughbourne. Why he wanted it hidden, I never found out, but I'd learned years before that asking questions only gets you answers you didn't really want to know.

"'Fetch it from the factory, and stow it down below,' he said. 'What the county ain't able to see, it ain't able to bitch about.'

"I knew exactly what he meant by *down below*. I wasn't happy about it, but eight years is a long time, and the memory had faded. Or so I thought. That same night I loaded up my truck with twenty oil drums of something I didn't want to think about, and took it to Hopman's mine.

"Now I ain't ashamed to tell you, I didn't want to go back down there into the dark. As I stood at the entrance to the shaft, the years seemed to fly away, as if they'd never happened, and suddenly I couldn't get the thought of the three missing men out of my mind. I wanted to just dump the waste at the entrance and head down here for a beer. But the business, such as it was, weren't doing too well, and I needed the old man's cash badly. So I loaded the drums on a cart, hitched it to the forklift, and headed down into the dark.

"That was when I found out just how busy old man Hopman had been in the intervening years. There's a proper warren down there, or at least there was back then, a nest of caverns, all crumbling, some with fresh cave-in material building up, others looking ready to drop at any minute…and this was thirty-odd years ago. God knows what it'll be like now. And that ain't the worst of it.

"I took them drums down as deep as I dared. And it were there that I found old man Hopman's secrets.

"He had some kind of operation going on down at the deepest level. There were generators, water barrels and refrigeration units…all kinds of shit. I reckoned he was building a bunker; remember that the Cold War was still going on, and some folks were just plain scared shitless. I had a look-see while I was there. There was a big iron door, obviously there to protect *something*, but it was locked tight. And I had started to get the heebie-jeebies by then anyway. I kept hearing somebody whispering to me, but when I looked around, there was never nobody there. After ten minutes of that crap, all I wanted to do was get back up top and have a drink...a lot of drinks.

"I did what the old man had told me to do. I followed the tracks to the deepest part, and found where I was supposed to leave the waste drums."

He paused again, took a deep drag of smoke and let it out very slowly. Fred saw something in the old man's eyes he hadn't seen before: pain. That, and a hint of fear.

"And here we get to the point of the story," Charlie finally said.

"Old man Hopman hadn't just been tunneling... he'd been dumping his industrial waste down there too; scores of barrels of the crap, some open and leaking, stacked willy-nilly in rough-hewed, crumbling caves. And the smell...I'll never forget it. It stung in the nose and throat like a rancid shit, and it took a whole bunch of beers later that night to get the taste of it out of my mouth.

"I'm telling you, son, it don't bear thinking about what might be down there by now, but I know one thing...we don't want it getting back up here."

* * *

Fred was quiet for a while, thinking about the thing he'd barely caught a glimpse of back in the hole; a white, slithering thing he'd only seen at the edge of his vision but suspected might be haunting his dreams that very night. Charlie, after his bout of being talkative, went back to a more normal period of silent drinking, which was fine by Fred. He was getting settled in for a long evening, and in truth was looking forward to the eventual oblivion the booze would bring.

Scraps of information came back from Hopman's Hollow over the next few hours, the gist of which was mostly more of the same. Big hole, getting bigger. There were other stories too; there would always be other stories where the Hopmans were concerned. Folks told of bodies that were there then were gone, of weird voices calling up out of the hole, and of strange diagrams seen on the walls and floor of the Hopman house just before it fell into the chasm. Fred and Charlie listened, then went back to drinking, both of them hoping to start to forget their own tribulations earlier that day.

But it was not to be.

The bar began to fill up, the crowd again full of excited chat about the *hole* which was the biggest thing to happen to the town in many a year. Once people heard that they'd been first on the scene, Fred and Charlie became the focus of some attention. Charlie got exasperated at first with the incessant questioning, but the pair of them quickly cottoned on to the fact that, as minor celebrities, they could squeeze a fair bit of free beer out of their story if they padded it out long enough.

Fred even started to enjoy himself, embellishing his story with new detail on each subsequent telling so that after an hour or so he had made himself out to be quite the hero. The one thing he didn't mention was the memory of the pale thing that had moved in the pit. He kept that locked away, and after a few more beers even started to forget about it completely.

# 6

Janet sat back from the microscope, then leaned forward for another look, just to make sure she had indeed seen what she thought she had. She had a sample on the slide, taken from the decayed matter she had gathered at the side of the hole.

It hadn't changed; it remained the same even on this, her third look. Where she'd expected to see cellular structure, maybe even blood cells, remnants of skin, some indication of organization, she saw instead merely a blob of undifferentiated protoplasm with nothing to indicate it had recently been part of a living body. There was no sign of mitochondria, nor of Golgi apparatus; no sign of much of anything. She was at a complete loss to explain it.

*Maybe this is an elaborate joke at my expense? Let's tease the outsider?*

"Well?" Bill Wozniak said. He sat across the table from her, cradling a coffee mug in his huge hands.

She couldn't believe the sheriff would be part of such a joke.

*And besides, creating a huge hole on the highway is taking it a bit far.*

She allowed herself a small smile at that, and Bill picked up on it.

"Have you found something?"

Janet shrugged.

"It's too badly degraded to tell much of anything," she said. "I'm afraid there's no easy explanation."

"Devils don't need no explaining," Bill said softly.

"Come on, Bill. Even you know that what we saw wasn't any such things as devils."

"I know no such thing," Bill replied. "And I'll tell you something else for nothing...I'm scared, Janet. Scared that there's going to be more of them before the night is out."

She didn't know how to answer that, and sat quietly. Bill spoke to fill the awkward silence that had developed.

"The sooner we get that hole filled in again, the happier I'll be."

"We need to investigate it further," Janet said.

Bill shook his head.

"Ain't gonna happen. I've got my orders from the town council. Close it up. Fill it with concrete if I have to. Just get rid of it."

Janet remembered the size of the hole as she'd last seen it. It was clearly a job well beyond the scope, and the budget, of the town's resources. She held her tongue though, as Bill was obviously in no mood for heeding the realities of the situation—not yet. That would come in the morning, when engineers, surveyors, builders and councilmen would all no doubt have their say, and at great length if precedent was anything to go by.

But for now, Bill was more concerned with the three bodies, or rather, the lack of them.

"We did see those demons, didn't we?" he asked. There was a plaintive tone in his voice, a memory of a younger, less confident man.

Janet nodded.

"We saw them. But as I told you, they weren't demons. They looked more like genetic mutations to me; some kind of mole rat, grown huge in a closed niche environment. I've heard of such things but…"

Bill cut off her speculation.

"Mole rats? That's not what I saw. Since when were mole rats bright red? Since when did mole rats have sharp horns? Since when…"

Now it was Janet's turn to interrupt.

"We're talking at cross purposes here, Bill. How about you tell me what you saw, see if I can make sense of this?"

He sipped at his coffee before answering, staring into the distance as he remembered.

"The hole weren't quite so big when I got there. This was just twenty minutes or so after Hopman called the ambulance for old Charlie. I left Deputy Watts with Hopman and did a tour of the damage. That was when I saw them, and I damned near shot myself in the foot getting my pistol out before I noticed they weren't moving. You say mole rats? I'm in no doubt of what they were. I told you already they were demons, and I ain't changing my story. The skin was bright red; it even looked kind of burnt. And the horns were stiff and sharp points. And those long fingers…with the talons and all? I'll never forget them, as long as I live."

*But it's not what I saw. There's something really hinky going on here.*

She thought it, but again held her tongue. The situation was fraught enough without adding another layer of confusion at this stage. She brewed up more coffee and steered the conversation away from the hole, for the moment. She knew it wouldn't be long before Bill was back worrying at it; that was his way. Just as it was her way to try to do something to keep him sane.

They'd grown close in recent months. People thought of them as rather an odd couple—the big bluff cop that knew everybody and the small thin doctor that everybody spoke to, but nobody knew. That was the way Janet liked it, or at least it had been until she met Bill. They'd clicked almost immediately, back more than a year ago, but Bill was still hurting then from the death of his wife. Janet was only now seeing signs that Bill might be getting over that, might be ready, if not to move on, to at least enjoy himself a little. Over coffee they made tentative plans to spend time together over the weekend.

"It's going to depend," Bill said. "If that hole keeps getting bigger, we might not be left with anywhere to go. It could turn out to be something the national media will take an interest in, and if that's the case, I ain't going to be getting any free time for a while. I've got a bad feeling about this one."

After Bill left, she went back to studying the slide under the lens. She still couldn't make any sense of it.

She refused to countenance Bill's talk of demons, but after examining the slide it was also clear that whatever she had seen, it certainly wasn't anything that fit into her conception of what made up a mammal.

Bill wasn't the only one with a bad feeling.

* * *

It was still worrying at her when she left the surgery later to make her way home. She didn't have far to go, and normally she enjoyed the slow stroll through the sleepy streets of the town. But now the place felt different; she couldn't put her finger on it, but it seemed as if the place had been given a dose of *hurry-up*. Everything seemed to be happening faster, people walked and talked with more purpose. The town had undergone a change, and she wasn't sure if she liked it.

Her own street was a case in point. On a normal evening she'd be one of the few out and about at this hour; most folks would just be sitting down to an evening meal, or crashing in front of the television. Tonight though, there was activity everywhere she looked. Clumps of people stood on corners or on porches, while others had even gone as far as starting to pack their pickups in preparation for making a getaway should it be needed. Children called and giggled excitedly and it felt more like the night before a carnival than anything else.

Switching on the television news didn't help matters. Bill had been right. The media were taking an interest. A too-tanned man of indeterminate age stood with his back to the hole in Hopman's Hollow.

He appeared almost gleeful at the prospect of more devastation.

"The sinkhole is estimated to be growing at two feet an hour," he said. "And it is by no means clear how much farther it will extend. It has already swallowed the home of local landowner and industrialist John Hopman, who tonight can only stand and observe as everything he has ever worked for falls away into the depths of the maw."

*At least they're not talking about devils.*

She listened for a while as she prepared a meal, but it was obvious that the reporters knew even less than Bill Wozniak did about the situation, and they were just filling up the airtime with idle speculation; everything from fault lines and mine subsidence, to earthquake and fracking damage. It did seem to be quite the story though, as, behind the reporter she was watching, she saw several other news crews, at least one of them *nationals*. Bill had been right to worry.

*This is going to get worse before it gets better.*

She didn't eat so much as shovel in fuel, and was surprised to look down and see the plate nearly empty. She stood over the garbage bin to dispose of the meager leftovers. And that's when she heard it again, a distant hum, like machinery running just at the reach of her hearing. She put a hand on the doorjamb, and felt a slight vibration thrum through the wood. Something seemed to slip inside her head, and she felt then tasted hot blood on her upper lip. A vise gripped her skull and started to tighten; a drummer taking up residence to pound out a beat that drowned everything else out. She staggered to the bathroom, smearing blood on door handles, sink and medicine cabinet before finding the painkillers. She took three, washed them down with water from the tap, then sat on the side of the bath, hand towel pressed to her nose, waiting for the drummer to tire, or her head to explode.

*Either will be a relief.*

* * *

Her doorbell rang just as the pain started to subside. Thankfully the nosebleed hadn't lasted long, and the mess it left behind was mainly confined to a blot on the hand towel and the bloody handprints she'd left in her path from the kitchen. She wiped the mess clean as she headed for the door and felt almost human again as she opened it.

Bill Wozniak stood outside on the sidewalk, a rueful grin on his face. He looked as tired as she felt, but she managed a small smile when she saw the tequila bottle in his hand.

"A nightcap for my lady?" he asked, and waved the bottle.

"Just the one," she replied. "It's been a long day."

"Don't I know it," he said. "And yes, it will just be the one. Then I'm heading back out to Hopman's Hollow. I left young Watts on patrol duty, and I can't let him stay there all night. He was getting twitchy the last time I called."

Over a glass of tequila—a large one for her, a smaller one for him, Bill brought her up to speed on the situation at Hopman's Hollow.

"It's getting bigger," he said. That was all he had

to say.

"How fast?" she asked.

"A couple of feet an hour. That don't sound too bad, but at fifty feet a day it ain't gonna be too long before it starts eating into some expensive real estate. That's when the squealing is really going to start."

A thought struck Janet.

"The *hum*...it's happening when the hole grows, isn't it?"

Bill smiled.

"I like a lady with plenty of smarts. Yep, I spotted that earlier. I was out there when the last *hum* started. It got rid of the news crews quick enough...first signs of nosebleeds and they were all off to the hospital squawking about chemical weapons."

"How about you? You okay?"

The big man tossed back the tequila, looked at the bottle, and shook his head sadly.

"Nothing a few more stiffeners wouldn't cure. But that'll have to wait. I've got to go. It's going to be a long night."

She spoke without thinking. "Want some company?" She wondered whether she'd misread him and spoken out of place, but his face lit up in a grin.

"That'll set a few tongues wagging in town. Ellen Simmons will surely be at your door first thing in the morning with a detailed report of proceedings. Are you ready for that?"

She grinned back. "As long as there's tequila, I'm ready for just about anything." She immediately felt heat rise on her cheeks and she started to stammer. "That didn't come out right. I didn't mean...you shouldn't...oh, shit."

Bill laughed loudly. "Don't worry, darling. I won't tell anybody. Your loose morals can remain a secret between the two of us."

He was still laughing as they went out to the parking bay where he'd parked the patrol car.

# 7

It had turned into one of *those* nights. Fred lost count of how many beers he'd necked and Charlie was already slumped in the corner of the bar nursing a JD and adamantly refusing to admit to being falling-over drunk.

At one point the *hum* started up again.

A girl in the corner screamed, two drunk teens passed out at their table, and some of the patrons had to leave, clutching fresh nosebleeds, but Fred was unaffected, whether by nature of previous exposure or just from being too goddamned drunk to care.

Charlie wiped fresh blood from his nose and threw Fred a mock salute.

"Here's to the end of the world," the older man shouted, and Fred grinned back at him, knocking back a JD and banging his glass on the bar for another. Things were starting to smooth over nicely. He had a buzz on that was only going to get stronger as the night went on; he'd already spent a wad of his eating money, but he was now past caring.

He got a second wind when a blonde arrived with free beer and questions.

"You're him, aren't you? You're the guy who saved the guy who fell down the hole on the guy's lawn?"

It took Fred several seconds to come to terms with the question, during which the blonde moved in on him, hustling her way onto the adjoining bar stool and leaning in close; close enough for Fred to feel the touch of her long hair on his arm. He started to pay closer attention.

"I was right, wasn't I? You're him?"

"I'm him."

"So what happened?" she said, and passed him a beer.

*A blonde and a beer; I can die happy.*

He took the beer, and answered as well as his befuddled mind would allow.

"Weren't nothing really," he started, and was immediately interrupted as she took his cigarette from him, sucked a long drag from it, and passed it back, placing it gently between his lips. It tasted sweeter somehow, and musky. Suddenly the booze didn't seem quite so important.

"I hear you're a hero?" she said, leaning closer still to whisper in his ear. He felt the heat of her breath on his cheek.

"Maybe I am at that," he replied, and gave her his best smile, to which she responded in kind. She bought him another beer while he told the story. He stuck to the truth, mostly, mainly because her deep blue eyes mesmerized him. Just looking into them made thinking a bit harder for him.

At some point he found himself retelling Charlie's story from earlier. When he got to the part about the three missing men, the blonde, *call-me-Tricia*, started to get excited.

"Oh…my…God. We should totally do a séance."

If it meant spending more time with a body to die for, and those blue eyes, Fred was all for it. She went on for quite a while, about *the other side* and *messages from the great beyond*, but all Fred remembered was how her breasts swelled against the thin fabric of her top.

* * *

The half an hour after that proved more than a bit fuzzy as he zoned in and out of a drunken stupor. He came back to reality grudgingly, sitting in an armchair in a trailer that was far too tidy to be his. A couple he didn't recognize sat in a sofa opposite him. The man, a portly guy in his thirties with a badly trimmed goatee, leaned over and handed Fred a beer.

"So, these three dead men, they're still hanging around?" the man said.

"Do I know you?" Fred asked.

The man laughed.

"Tricia invited me over for the séance. Tell me it's true…these dead men from the mine, and the hole and…"

Fred felt as if he'd been cut loose from reality. He had no memory of leaving the bar, no idea what he was doing in this stranger's trailer. To cover his confusion he lit a cigarette, getting it going at only the second attempt. He was saved having to answer by a voice from the adjoining kitchen area.

"That's what Fred said," the blonde called back. She came through into the main living area. "Found it."

*It* proved to be a bashed-up Ouija board in a tattered box. *The Mysterious Mystifying Oracle* it said on the front. It looked innocuous enough, but a chill crept into Fred's spine, and suddenly he was thinking again—of lost men, and pale things slithering in dark pits. He chugged down half the beer, spilling some on his shirt, a small price to pay for managing to dispel the dark thoughts, at least for the moment.

Tricia laid the board on the coffee table in the center of the room, then sat down at Fred's feet. When he felt the warmth of her back on his legs, he started to think maybe he should stop drinking and pay attention again for a while.

She unfolded the board. It had obviously seen a lot of use. The lettering was scratched and faded in places, and somebody had scrawled all over it in red ink at some time in the past. But just looking at it gave Fred a funny feeling in his stomach that couldn't be put down to the booze.

"I don't know about this..." he started, but stopped when the blonde put a warm hand on his knee.

"Just tell them, Fred," Tricia said. "Tell them the story. Just the way you told me. Please?"

In truth he struggled to remember if he'd put any embellishment into the tale on its earlier telling, but it didn't seem to matter. The others lapped it up as if he were relaying the Ten Commandments.

"As Charlie tells it, they're still down there, somewhere. The bodies were never found," he said, pushing down another chill that threatened to have him shivering.

"We should totally try to contact them," the blonde said.

"Maybe they can tell us what's causing the hole in the hollow?" the man on the sofa said.

*Shit, I might be drunk, but at least I'm not stupid.*

Fred started to move, intending to get up and leave, but Tricia pressed her back more firmly against his legs and squirmed. Fred sat back in the chair and chugged some beer.

*Let them have some fun. Nothing will come of it, and maybe I can get her alone for a time later.*

"You've done this before then?" Fred asked. Tricia turned to look at him and he felt her breasts jiggle against his knee, distracting him so much he nearly dropped his beer.

"Not since I was a kid," she said. "But it works more often than not."

"What do you mean, *works*?"

"We can talk to the spirits. Get messages from those who have passed on."

"Bullshit."

She smiled to let him see that she wasn't offended.

"No, really. It answers questions. There's a theory that it all comes from our own subconscious and we move the glass by micromovements in our fingers controlled by our unconscious minds but..."

She stopped. Fred had zoned out again, losing interest halfway through her sentence, and she'd obviously noticed. Once again, it didn't seem to affect her good humor. She smiled at him again, then turned back towards the table.

"Let's do it."

Fred felt an almost palpable sense of loss as her weight lifted from his legs. She only went as far as the coffee table, setting an upturned glass in the middle of the board. She patted the floor beside her. "Come on down here," she said. "We all need to be touching the glass or it won't work."

Fred got off the armchair, and his legs wobbled alarmingly under him. He tried to kneel, overbalanced, and almost head-butted the coffee table before managing to right himself. Tricia laughed and steadied him with a hand on his shoulder. She took the beer from him and put it to one side.

"I've got a bottle of rye in the cupboard," she said. "We can start to party soon. But first, I *really* want to do this. Please?"

*I never could resist a blue-eyed woman.*

He nodded, carefully, unsure of how steady he was. Her answering smile improved matters considerably. He made sure he wasn't about to fall over and settled in at Tricia's side. The other two moved to take up position around the coffee table.

"What now?" Fred asked. He was starting to regret ever leaving The Roadside, but he just had to look to his left and see Tricia to remind him why he'd allowed himself to be brought here. Even if he couldn't remember doing it, his instincts would always follow a blonde, no matter how drunk he was.

"Now we stay quiet," she replied. "Just put a finger on the glass, and let me ask all the questions."

Fred did as he was told. In truth, he had no idea what was going on, and just hoped to see it through as fast as possible so he could find out what Tricia's idea of a *party* might be. The other two present, whose names Fred still didn't know, seemed as serious as Tricia about this séance, so Fred let them have their head. He kept a finger on the glass in the center of the board, but with the other hand he continued to smoke a cigarette and swig from the beer bottle.

The glass under his finger on the board felt cold to the touch, as if it had just been taken out of a fridge.

"Is anybody there?" Tricia said, in a tone so solemn and fake that Fred let out a snort of laughter.

"Ain't nobody here but us chickens."

That got him a look that told him to behave, and a smile that reminded him of the possibility of a *party*. Suitably chastised, he kept quiet as she went back to concentrating on the glass. Her tongue poked wetly from her lips, and Fred decided, yet again, that he might stay a bit longer.

"Is anybody there?" she asked.

Fred resisted an almost overwhelming urge to speak up again.

The room fell quiet.

"Is it getting colder?" the man opposite him whispered. "I'm sure it's getting colder."

All Fred felt was a cramp, slowly spreading in his left leg; that, and an insistent urge to pee.

"Is anybody there?" Tricia asked again.

The glass moved, slowly at first, with a jerk, then more smoothly, centering itself over the faded *YES* on the board. To Fred it felt like the glass was hovering under his finger, moving like a flat-bottomed stone on smooth ice.

"You moved it," the man across the table said. Tricia was looking wide-eyed at the glass. She shook her head.

"Not me."

Fred was too shocked to answer, and the girl on his other side merely sat gaping, open-mouthed in wonder. Before anyone could speak, the glass moved again. It felt like it floated under his finger, scarcely touching the board at all. It circled the inner part of the board counterclockwise, as if waiting.

"Ask it something," the man whispered.

*Please don't.*

"Who are you?" Tricia said, softly.

The glass moved over the board. Tricia spoke the letters where it paused.

"F...R...E...D...I...S...D...E...A...D."

"What the hell does that mean?" the man opposite said. Fred scarcely heard him. He'd already read the message, and his mind was filled again with pictures of a pale slithering thing in deep darkness. His heartbeat pounded in his ears and a sudden nausea gripped his guts. He stood, too fast, scattering the Ouija board, the glass and two beers across the trailer floor as he made for the washroom.

* * *

He only just made it. He emptied his stomach in one heave, tasting beer coming back up. Another spasm hit, then another. Every time he thought he was done, he saw the glass move in his mind's eye, spelling out the letters.

F...R...E...D...I...S...D...E...A...D

*What the fuck is going on here?*

He had no answers. He stayed in the washroom for a while until his guts eased and he felt he could move without chucking up.

*Screw this. I'm going home.*

But by the time he returned to the main living area, the other three had the board set up, and the glass was once again moving smoothly across the board.

"You okay?" Tricia asked. She looked up and smiled. That was enough to get him to sit beside her again.

*But there ain't no way I'm touching that glass.*

Tricia handed him a notebook with messages written in a scrawled hand.

"I think it's them," she whispered. "I think it's your men from down the mine."

She went back to the board with the others as Fred read the call-and-response in the scribbled notes, the knot in the pit of his stomach getting tighter with every line.

"Who are you?"

*"FredJoeGeorge."*

"Where are you?"

*"Fred is dead."*

"Where are you?"

*"With Fred."*

"Are you in Hopman's Hollow?"

*"Fred is. Fred is dead."*

"Did you cause the hole to collapse?"

*"Fred did. Fred is dead."*

Tricia gasped loudly and Fred looked up from the

notepad. The three others stared, open-mouthed and wide-eyed, at the board. The glass spun under their fingers, faster and faster, in a tight circle around the word *NO.* Without warning, it cracked and fell in three pieces to the board.

For a second everything went completely quiet and still.

"What just happened?" the man across the table said. Tricia looked at Fred.

"I think it was them."

Fred lit a fresh smoke, having to force his hands to stay steady.

"You three have just spooked yourselves. There ain't no such thing as ghosts."

"Are you shitting me?" the man across the table said. "After what we've just seen?"

The lights in the room all dimmed at once, and the background hum that had been there from the refrigerator weakened and dulled to little more than a whisper. Shadows gathered in the corners, darkening as the lights faded further. The trailer vibrated, thrumming like a tuning fork, sending tremors up through Fred's body. He felt wetness at his lip and tasted fresh blood. The jackhammer started up again behind his right eye.

*Oh, crap. I think we're in trouble.*

Tricia looked down at the dribble of blood that ran from her chin down to her cleavage. Fred found he was no longer quite so interested in the contents of the top. The man across from them wiped at his nose and left a bloody smear across his cheek. The girl beside him sat, leaning slightly forward, dripping a steady patter of droplets onto the glass tabletop, where they pooled and started to run towards the broken shards of the drinking glass.

"What is *this* shit?" Tricia said.

No one had time to reply.

The floor lurched beneath them. The girl across the table screamed—the first sound he'd heard from her all night. Tricia grabbed his hand, hard enough to bring a flare of pain as the old trailer squealed and tipped up, kitchen end first. The four of them tumbled and rolled, as if caught in a washing machine's cycle.

* * *

Despite the booze, Fred was the first to react as the trailer came to a stop with a thud. He had a mental flash, an image of Hopman's septic tank tumbling down into the black chasm, and had a good idea what was happening to them.

"Everybody out. Now!" he shouted, and headed for the door, even as the trailer lurched again and tipped up to a thirty-degree angle. Loose furniture slid across the floor, and there was a clatter and crash from the scullery as the kitchenware scattered.

The other man crouched in the fetal position by the sofa, moaning piteously. The two women were right behind Fred as he opened the door. The front end of the trailer took a fresh dive downwards, threatening to knock them off their feet again. Bottles, glasses, television and coffee table all flew in the air to crash and break against the kitchen wall. The hunched man slid, almost comically slowly, across the floor, mewling like a frightened kitten as he went.

Tricia made a move to go to help him, but Fred pushed her out the door.

"I'll get him. Just go."

Outside all was dark. Screams echoed through the night, accompanied by a crashing, tearing cacophony of breaking glass and twisting metal. Whatever was happening, it wasn't confined to this trailer. But there was no time to dwell on that.

The quiet girl had already leapt, still silent, out into the dark. Tricia turned in the doorway and held out a hand towards Fred.

"Come on," she shouted. "It's going over."

Fred reached for her. The man across the room wailed again.

"Don't leave me!"

Fred looked at Tricia's hand, then across at the terrified man in the corner.

*Like a deer in the headlights.*

"I can't leave him," Fred said. "You go. I'm right behind you."

He waited until Tricia leapt from the doorway before heading across the room, almost having to climb as the trailer took another lurch.

*Out of time. I'm not going to reach him.*

"Come here!" he shouted at the man.

The man wailed again, a wordless cry of fear. Fred yelled back at him.

"If you don't come here right now, I'm going to kick ten grades of shit out of you."

That finally got the other man moving. He got unsteadily to his feet and headed for Fred in a sideward shuffle. The trailer squealed and rolled slightly, throwing the men together. They clasped hands and headed for the doorway, reaching it just as the trailer stood up, almost vertical on its front end.

"Jump," Fred shouted. The man seemed to have gained some courage from somewhere. He leapt out into the darkness. Fred tried to follow, but was caught off balance by another jolt of the trailer. A scream came from outside, and then the trailer started to tip over. Fred grabbed for the edge of the door, managed to get a hold and pulled himself upright.

"Jump," someone shouted. He didn't need to be told twice. He leapt into darkness, just as the trailer fell away from beneath him.

He heard a crash, far below, but he was too busy scrambling for footing. He managed to get clear of the falling trailer, but had jumped, not onto solid ground, but against the crumbling wall of a newly formed hole. For a horrible second he thought he might tumble down to join the debris in the pit, but then he found some purchase, and pulled himself up, clambering out of the hole. He rolled aside, panting with exertion and trying not to throw up what little remained in his gut.

Another scream came from somewhere nearby, one that was quickly cut off, leaving behind only silence.

He got unsteadily to his feet and looked around, disoriented.

"Don't just stand there," Tricia shouted. "Run."

She was ten yards to his left, standing with the other two. Fred immediately saw that he stood in a precarious situation. The ground at his right was still falling away into the darkness as a new hole grew. And it wasn't the only one. Fresh screams rose from all around the trailer park, and even from where he stood, Fred saw that at least a dozen of the mobile homes had been swallowed, lost somewhere in the deep. Off to his left another leaned at a precarious angle and, before he could move, tumbled away out of sight.

"Get over here," Tricia shouted. She sounded almost hysterical. "Right fucking now."

He started to move towards the trio...just as the ground collapsed in front of him. He managed to keep his balance and leapt to safety.

The others weren't so fortunate.

The wall of the new hole slid in one huge slab of earth with them on top of it, straight down into the blackness.

The last thing Fred saw as he looked down was the blonde mop of hair, disappearing into the gloom as Tricia, and her friends, fell screaming into the dark.

# 8

Janet and Bill were parked just off road to the west of Hopman's Hollow. They sat on the bonnet, sharing the last of the sheriff's coffee from the large travelling mug he kept in the car. It had gone lukewarm, but Janet didn't mind that, as long as the brew was strong, and Bill liked his coffee strong enough to stand a spoon in.

A clear sky hung overhead, and a crescent moon was just coming up over the trees. It might almost have been peaceful, if it wasn't for the almost constant sound of earth falling away into the growing hole. They were over a hundred yards from the edge, parked at one of the roadblocks Bill had asked to be set up, and Janet still didn't feel quite safe.

*But I'm not leaving Bill out here alone.*

They'd both been quiet for several minutes, but this was no awkward silence.

"We should do this more often," she said.

Bill laughed.

"What, stand guard over a hole that threatens to swallow the town?"

She punched his arm, playfully.

"You know what I mean. It's nice to get some peace and quiet."

Bill nodded and looked up at the stars spread overhead.

"Do you ever wonder? What it's all about? What it's all for?"

"Having deep thoughts, Bill? It's not like you."

He took a while to answer.

"It was seeing those *devils* that did it. I always had some sort of faith, a weak one, but it's there. But seeing those—things—has made me think. How about you?"

She had a speech pre-prepared; one honed in long, slightly drunken, conversations at medical college, back when she'd tried to engage in debate with her more religious classmates. She brought it out again, for the first time in years, but she remembered it almost by heart.

"Faith? I put my faith in science. Life for me is an opportunity to create meaning by my deeds, my actions and how I manage my way through the short part of infinity I'm given to operate in. And once my life is finished, my atoms will go back to forming other interesting configurations with those of other people, animals, plants and anything else that happens to be around, as we all roll along in one big, ever-changing, universe."

"No God?" Bill asked softly.

She shook her head. "None needed. Not for me."

"Then I pity you," Bill said, and Janet felt a flash of anger that she pushed down. Back at college she would have vented at his point, letting loose a diatribe against *big sky fairies* and *superstitious claptrap.* But that wasn't anything Bill needed to hear.

*Not now, not tonight.*

"Look up there," Janet said. "Some of that starlight blazed billions of years ago, from billions of stars in billions of galaxies. I'm not so conceited as to think that all of that was created just for the benefit of folks that live on a tiny speck of blue and white tucked away in a small corner in the middle of nowhere. We folks have only been here for a tiny fraction of the lifetime of the universe, and given the way we're going, I don't think we'll be around long enough to make too much of an impact on the grand scheme of things. But some of my atoms will be around long enough to be there at the death of our own star. I rather like that idea."

Bill was quiet for a long time.

"Do you think there's anyone else out there?" he said.

"If there is, I doubt they're anything like us. Evolution happens through a process of species adapting to ecological niches, and ecology is too highly determined by place. Our planet's ecosystem is highly adapted to living eighty or so million miles away from a yellow sun, with a captive, close moon. There won't be that many others just like us...but I'm sure there's other life out there somewhere. The universe is too big to be empty."

"But that's something you take on faith?" Bill asked.

It was her turn to laugh.

"I suppose it is."

*It's faith based on a good scientific guess. But that's a discussion for another night.*

She felt a chill as a breeze got up. She didn't feel tired, despite the long day. Years of medical training meant she was well used to pulling all-nighters, something doctors shared with cops. She held tight to Bill's arm, and hoped their differing views on faith were not going to grow into a problem.

She was still mulling that over when she felt the squad car tremble beneath them, and heard a distant, but distinct, hum. Her headache kicked in again, and there was fresh blood at her nostrils. It wasn't an outpouring like the gush that had hit her back in her home; the bleed was little more than a dribble. But the headache was much worse, like a vise had been clamped on her skull and tightened until the bone was close to cracking.

"We should go," Bill said, his voice seeming to come from a great distance. Janet didn't answer. Her gaze was fixed on Hopman's Hollow. At first she only thought she'd seen movement there, the barest hint of something flickering. Then it got brighter, and more persistent.

A pulsing blue light rose out of the hole. It grew brighter still until it threw harsh shadows over the whole area. Something rose out of the deep and lifted into the air, hovering above them, a steely-blue saucer that hummed and throbbed before departing up, fast as a blink, into the blackness of the stars. They watched it go until its light was too faint to distinguish among the stars.

A voice whispered at her ear.

*Do you think there's anyone else out there?*

She turned to see who had spoken. There was no one there. There was just the wind in the trees, and darkness at the side of the road.

"What is going on here?" Bill said.

Janet didn't have an answer.

* * *

She was still trying to process what had happened when the squad car radio squawked into action seconds later. Young Watts was on the other end, and he sounded terrified.

"Sheriff? You'd best get back to town. We've got a big problem around the trailer park."

"What kind of problem?"

"Best you see for yourself. But hurry."

Janet got into the passenger seat without being asked. Bill spun the car into a screeching turn and pointed it back at town. Even from here on the farthest outskirts it was clear there was indeed a real problem. Half the town sat in darkness, the shadowed area pockmarked with the red flare and flicker of flames. Something exploded, with the *crump* of the bang reaching them a second later. A pall of gray smoke rose before getting lost in the blackness of the night.

*Are we under some kind of attack?*

Bill didn't hesitate. He sped along the highway and took the first possible turn-off towards the affected area, throwing the car into the corner so much that the back end started to drift, and he only just managed to hold them on the road.

"Steady on, Bill. The town's not going anywhere."

"I'm not so sure about that."

They only got fifty more yards before he had to screech to a halt. There was no road ahead of them, just a gaping hole. The headlights showed only darkness ahead, with no indication of the extent of this new collapse. Bill got out of the car.

"Stay here," he said.

*Yeah, like that's going to happen.*

She got out and joined him. The hole at their feet seemed bottomless, falling away almost vertically below them. Janet felt her head swim, and her legs start to go out from under her. Bill pulled her away, only a foot or so, but enough for the vertigo to subside. Smoke and the smell of burning rubber rose from the hole, but there was no indication what was down there. Janet was still trying to gauge the size of the thing when Bill let out a soft expletive.

She looked up and followed his gaze.

It looked like the whole north end of town was gone. At the farthest part away from where they stood, where the trailer park had been, several fresh fires burned. A scream came on the wind, quickly cut off. There were some trailers remaining, a handful at most, but there had been more than a hundred earlier, most of them with families, with children.

Between what was left of the trailer park and where Bill and Janet stood, the town looked like it had been bombed. It was almost too dark to see, for the street lighting had failed, but there were enough fires to show a vision of hell.

What had once been three neat streets of well-maintained houses and gardens was now a jumble of broken timber, twisted roofing and mangled plumbing. Water sprayed high from burst pipes, small fires burned exposed drapery and bedding and electricity sparked where downed wires slithered like snakes across the rubble. Janet saw what she took to be a doll lying on the remains of a sofa, bent and broken. But it was no doll; it was a child, no more than five years old, neck broken and discarded like a rag by whatever disaster had befallen the town.

She hadn't noticed that Bill had left her side, and was now on the squad car radio.

"We need backup out here. Everything we've got. And call County, the National Guard...anybody you can think of."

Somebody replied, too faintly for Janet to hear at this distance.

"No...an ambulance and the fire truck won't be enough," Bill shouted in reply. "Get everybody out of bed and down here. And do it now."

The big man was red in the face and shaking, whether in fury or grief Janet couldn't tell, but he was working himself up into quite a state. Janet was about to head over to try and calm the sheriff when she heard a weak cry, then two more, from her left.

"Help. Please. Help us."

She picked her way over to the edge of the hole and looked down. It was dark down there, but the glare from the car headlights behind her gave her just enough light to see by. A family of two adults and three kids were making their slow way up the precarious slope. They looked like something from a war newsreel; mud-stained, pale with the wide, unbelieving eyes of victims.

And there was blood. Lots of it.

Just looking down brought back a fresh spell of dizziness. She looked to Bill, but the big man was still on the radio, still trying to impress the severity of the situation on his subordinates. Janet turned her back to the hole and edged down over the lip, keeping her gaze on the wall of earth in front of her face as she went down, her doctor's instincts overriding all caution. Luckily the ground here was more clay than earth and although that meant it was hard going reaching the family, it meant less likelihood of the ground giving way beneath her. Her feet sucked and threatened to stick. She dug her toes into the thick soil and lowered herself, inch by inch.

"Help," a voice called out, much closer now. She chanced a look down. She was only a foot or so above the struggling family. She allowed herself to slide down to where the small group still struggled upward.

"Thank God," the father whispered. "I thought we were the only ones left."

The man looked near exhaustion. Janet took the weight of a young girl who was slumped, exhausted, against him. That gave the man a fresh jolt of energy, and he was able to free himself and another child from the thick clay. Between them, Janet and the man started to make faster headway, and Bill's appearance at the top of the slope soon meant they were all able to pull everyone out of the hole and roll aside, tired, panting, but alive.

* * *

It took her several seconds to catch her breath. Bill helped her to her feet, looked her up and down and smiled grimly.

"Looking good on date night," he said.

Janet looked down. She was caked, from neck to toe, in clinging gray mud.

"You can help me wash it off later," she said, and turned away as Bill's mouth fell open in astonishment.

She spent the next ten minutes tending to the family. Apart from superficial cuts and bruises the kids were little the worse for wear, but the mother had a bruise the size of an egg above her left eye, and seemed confused, possibly concussed. The husband had deep lacerations along the back of both hands that she was able to bandage using the first-aid kit in the squad car, and she was just getting round to a nasty gash at his thigh when the first ambulance turned up.

Getting the man into it turned into somewhat of a pantomime as first he refused to leave his family, then the family refused to let him go without them, and the whole thing turned into a shouting and screaming match until Bill finally lost it.

"Just bloody go. All of you," he shouted, the force of his personality so strong it shocked everybody into obedient silence.

"Nice job, Mr. Shouty," Janet said as the ambulance, with the whole family crammed inside, headed out.

"Ain't gonna be a lot of quiet around here tonight," Bill replied grimly. "Best get used to it."

* * *

Over the next half an hour they started to get some idea of the scale of the disaster. Janet spent most of the time tending to a steady trail of walking wounded. They arrived in dribs and drabs, picking their way through wreckage and around collapsed ground. Bill was somewhere out in the night with his deputies and three paramedics, assessing the damage and looking for more survivors. Janet felt more tense and nervous with every minute that passed. She tried to keep her mind on her job, to focus on the patients, but the thought of Bill out in the dark, with the chance of a fresh collapse at any time, had her nerves frayed to breaking point. She almost sobbed when the big man walked out of the ruins.

He had three kids with him, all of them in shock. He sat on the squad car hood, more tired than she'd ever seen him, caked head to toe in grime, soot and blood while Janet assessed the kids.

*They'll live. But they might never be the same.*

She packed them off in another ambulance before turning to Bill.

"How bad is it?" she asked.

She thought he wasn't going to answer at first, and when he did, it was in a small, almost childlike voice far removed from his usual confident tone.

"A full third of the town's gone. Just gone…fallen into new holes. The worst of the damage is over at the trailer park. We've got over two hundred folks missing, and that's over and above the thirty bodies we've recovered from what little wreckage was left."

*Two hundred?*

Janet's mind could scarcely take it in. The big man looked ready to burst into tears, and she feared that if he did, she might join him.

*We're not equipped for this.*

"We need to get the authorities here in force. And we need them now."

Bill wiped a hand across his brow, smearing a scar of mud across his forehead.

"I've made the call. They say they're on their way. God knows when they'll get here though."

Janet looked around her. The area where they'd stopped the squad car was now a makeshift recovery center, a hubbub of medics, cops and volunteer townsfolk. And patients...an ever-growing body of wounded and shocked.

"I need to get these folks inside," Janet said. "And if there's going to be more, we'll need somewhere with space for them all."

That seemed to get Bill moving. He stood up, straightened, and was once more the strong cop she knew.

"I'll get them to open up the church hall. That's in the area that still has power, so we'll get heat, running water, and someplace we can get some food into folks. Big enough for you?"

"It'll do. For now."

* * *

Bill had the church hall opened, and Janet helped with getting it set up as an emergency center. Supplies were few and far between, even after scavenging what they could from the police department, the supermarket and shops, and Janet's own surgery. Bill had put out calls for urgent emergency assistance to County but Janet knew all too well the glacial speed at which local, and hospital management in particular, came to decisions, and she wasn't holding out too much hope of getting any help before morning. She had to make the best of what they had. With over a hundred walking wounded, and more coming in all the time, it was obvious the supplies weren't going to stretch too far.

That wasn't the only cause for concern. Many of the wounded had their heads down, hunched over their cell phones, attempting to make calls. Nobody could get a signal. One teenager wailed, inconsolably, as if he'd lost a member of his family. An elderly gentleman that Janet didn't know said what was on a lot of their minds.

"What if it's like this all over? What if the whole country, the whole world, is going to pot? Maybe there is no help out there."

Janet had her hands full, not only with treating wounds, but in trying to calm an increasingly agitated group.

"Can we move them?" Bill asked when she expressed her concerns on one of his return visits.

"What, all of them?"

He nodded.

"I ain't too happy staying here, what with the possibility of a fresh cave-in at any moment."

"You think that's likely?"

"You think it isn't?"

He had her there. She'd put such thoughts to the

back of her mind while treating the wounded, but now that the back of that task was broken, she had time to think...too much time.

"You've got a point. I take it you have a plan?" she asked.

"I think we need to evacuate," Bill said. "At least until we can check that it'll be safe to return. If I sequester all the school buses, taxis and trucks in the area, we should be able to ferry everybody out at once."

"Does everybody know?"

Bill nodded.

"I had what men I could spare going round knocking on doors. A lot of them have left already, and the rest know that we're gathering around here. I just have to round up enough drivers for the buses."

"I'll do what I can here to get us ready for moving," she replied. "Most are mobile enough, and fit to make a journey. As long as it's not too far."

Bill whispered, so that only she could hear.

"That's what I'm worried about. How far do we need to go? I plan to head for the county hospital, as long as we can get out of town without mishap. How's that for a plan?"

She smiled thinly.

"It'll do, until something better comes along. A bit like you, really."

He surprised her by taking her into his arms and hugging her tight.

"Don't be going anywhere until I get back," he said, and headed out into the wounded town.

# 9

Fred was back on a stool at The Roadside, drunk, but not as drunk as he wanted to be. A steady stream of distraught and bewildered townsfolk arrived in search of something, anything, to block out the sights they had just seen. Others had gone to see what they could do to help out at the church hall, and Fred felt a pang of guilt as he watched them leave…but not enough to shift him from his stool. He knew that if he saw even one blonde, he wouldn't be able to do much except weep, maybe scream. He tossed some beer down after his latest JD and ordered another of each.

The television was on, turned low, tuned in to a game show. There had been a brief story earlier, but that had only covered the first collapse at Hopman's Hollow. As yet, news of the disaster around the trailer park hadn't hit the media, but Fred knew that when it did, a shit storm of epic proportions would rage over the town. He wasn't sure he wanted any part of it.

*I should up and go. Right now. Ain't got nothing to my name but the clothes I'm wearing and my wallet. But that's enough to be getting on with.*

He stayed in his seat and lit up a fresh smoke. The bar was a safe place, a source of comfort; always had been. It was where he came when his mom died, where he came after the accident that almost put him in jail for a spell. He came here when he wanted to forget, and tonight he had plenty of memories that needed to be hidden.

Luckily nobody wanted to talk to him. The story seekers from earlier had all moved on, and Hopman's Hollow was now merely a prelude to the bigger tale unfolding. Maybe if they knew that Fred had also been out in the trailer park tonight, maybe then he might be the focus of attention once more.

*But I've got enough folks killed for one night. The only thing I'm opening my mouth for now is to pour more booze inside.*

Amazingly, Charlie was still upright, and still drinking. His head wound was less raw-looking than it had been, and he had much of his color back. He stood from his place in the corner and negotiated the bar like a sailor in rough seas before sitting next to Fred and ordering more JD for them both.

"You've done seen something, ain't you, boy?" Charlie said, slurring his words, but not enough to make him unintelligible. Fred said nothing, just sucked smoke and tried to clear his mind. The whispers from the television seemed to speak straight to him.

*Fred is dead.*

He jerked up his head and looked at the screen. The game show host smiled inanely back at him.

Try as he might, he couldn't make any sense of what had happened back in the trailer. It was almost as if the séance had led directly to the formation of the new holes, but he refused to believe that. He also tried to refuse to believe that he had seen the glass float and spin above the Ouija board, but that was taking a bit more effort to eradicate, and was going to need more booze.

*A lot more booze.*

Charlie wasn't done with him yet.

"Fess up, boy. Something's got you spooked, ain't it?"

Fred sucked smoke and let it out slowly. He knew Charlie wasn't one to let something drop once he got an idea into his head.

*Besides, he might even know something that'll help me make sense of what happened.*

"What were the names of the three men that went missing down the mine?" he asked.

"Why do you want to know?" Charlie said, his confusion writ large on his face.

"Just tell me," Fred said. He kept his eyes on the television, not trusting himself to look at the older man.

"Fred Miller, George Tomkins and Joseph O'Brien," Charlie said. "God rest their souls."

*FredJoeGeorge. He told me before. He must have told me before.*

"Why do you want to know?" Charlie asked

again, but Fred didn't reply. He threw a shot of JD down his throat, feeling the heat burn to his stomach and a fuzzy haze grow larger in his head.

*That's right. Kill those brain cells. Murder them.*

But no matter how much JD he put down, the images kept bubbling back to the surface, the last one in particular, of the blonde, Tricia, falling, screaming into darkness.

The television whispered to him again.

*Fred is dead.*

He threw his shot glass at the screen, drunkenness affecting his aim enough that the glass hit a timber some two feet to the right of the television and shattered. All noise in the bar cut off, and everyone turned. Fred felt their gaze, like a weight on the back of his head. He didn't have to turn round to know he'd just become that which he'd tried to avoid. He had their attention.

"That's enough for you, Fred," the barman said. "Go home and sleep it off."

Fred laughed hollowly.

"I ain't got no home to go to," he shouted, too loud in the quiet bar. "Damned hole sucked it right up." He dropped his head to rest it on the table. "Sucked her right up," he whispered.

The bar patrons, realizing that no more outbursts were forthcoming, went back to their conversations. Fred suddenly ached for company...blonde company. He closed his eyes, but immediately opened them again, his mind full of visions of a fair mop of hair falling, deeper and deeper, screaming into the dark.

He felt a hand on his shoulder and turned to stare into Charlie's concerned face. The older man looked suddenly sober.

"Tell me, son. Tell me everything."

That was all it took. Fred started to speak, and the whole story came out in a rush of words and bitter tears.

"They were there, Charlie," he said near the end. "At least one of them was there. I felt him, saw him move the glass, sure as eggs is eggs."

Charlie was quiet for long seconds.

"There ain't no such things as ghosts, lad," he said. "You know that."

Fred nodded.

"Before tonight I'd have said the same thing. But I know what I saw, Charlie. And I ain't about to unsee it."

Charlie handed him another JD and sucked smoke before answering.

"I saw plenty of things back in 'Nam I ain't never gonna forget," he said. "Saw plenty of men, good and bad, die horrible, messy deaths. And not one of them ever came back. Packets of blood and shit; that's all we are, son. Ain't no sense in thinking otherwise."

Fred didn't reply. The events of the night were starting to fade as the booze finally took hold, but he couldn't allow himself to give in to its seduction, not tonight.

*Not when I ain't got nowhere to go when the bar closes.*

* * *

Bill Wozniak arrived some time later. He walked straight over to Fred and Charlie. Fred winced and kept his head down. The sheriff had been the one that took the call the night of Fred's accident. The big man had cut Fred a break that night and helped out with some creative writing of the official report. That was enough to keep him out of jail, but Fred still felt uncomfortable around the officer, fearing that the favor might be called in at any moment.

"You sober, Charlie?" the sheriff said. "I need a bus driver and we're coming up short."

"Sure thing," Charlie said, tried to stand and staggered into Fred. The sheriff raised an eyebrow. Charlie straightened up.

"I stood up a mite too fast there, Sheriff. But I'll be fine."

The older man threw a mock salute, and staggered slightly again.

The sheriff sighed, but handed Charlie a bundle of heavy keys.

"These are Joe's for his school bus," he said. "We ain't found Joe."

He didn't say any more, but Fred saw it in his eyes. Joe was another one who he wouldn't be seeing again anytime soon.

Charlie took the keys, dropped them, and almost fell on his face trying to pick them up.

"I got no right letting you near a vehicle in that state," the sheriff said. "But this is an emergency. Get some coffee in you, fast. We're moving out and taking the wounded and the kids first. Bring her to the church hall in twenty. And Fred?"

Fred looked up.

"I'm trusting you to make sure he gets that bus down to where it's needed. Okay?"

Fred nodded, although the last thing he felt like

doing was heading out into the dark.

*Looks like that favor has just been called in.*

*   *   *

Main Street was as busy as he'd ever seen it. Several of the stores were open for business, and people with laden trolleys filled cars and pickups. It looked like folks were preparing for the apocalypse.

*And maybe that ain't too far from the truth of the matter.*

Even with all the commotion in and around the stores, it was hard to imagine the scale of the tragedy that had unfolded, and might still be ongoing, over at the trailer park. But all Fred had to do was look in the faces of the folks on the street to see that this was a situation that looked to get a lot worse before it got better.

Charlie slugged down coffee from a travelling mug and passed it to Fred. Tony had made it as strong as he could get it, and Fred felt his heart rate go up a notch as it hit his system. The fresh air threatened to go to his head, but he remembered the look he'd got from Big Bill.

*I'm trusting you.*

Tonight wasn't the night to be testing the limits of the sheriff's faith in him. He took Charlie by the arm and started to frog-march him up the road. They left Main Street and headed up the hill towards the spot where Joe normally parked his bus. Several families in the street were in the process of packing belongings into pickups, but not as many as Fred might have expected. Many of the houses were quiet and dark, either because the inhabitants had already moved on or, as Fred believed, they had stuck their heads in the sand and were refusing to see what was happening on the other side of town. It was something he'd got used to over the years of living here. A lot of folks in this area could give ostriches lessons in sticking their heads in the sand. Fred didn't get over this way much; too heady for his liking, with manicured lawns, trimmed hedges and perfectly painted porches. It made his trailer look like what it had been—little more than a shed with a bed—and it reminded him how far down he'd fallen in the few short years since leaving a home remarkably like the ones he now walked past with eyes averted.

Thinking of the trailer threatened to revive images from earlier in the evening. He pushed them down and concentrated on getting Charlie where he needed to go.

"Not far now," Charlie said, as if trying to convince them to keep going. The older man staggered again, and Fred had to take his weight to stop him from falling. Fred wasn't sure either of them was in any way capable of driving a bus.

*At least there's not much traffic to contend with.*

As if in reply to his thoughts, the radio in a parked truck at the curbside crackled into life.

"Fred is. Fred is dead."

Charlie looked confused.

"Did you hear that?"

Fred didn't reply. Nothing he could say would help. Instead he walked faster, half dragging Charlie up the road. As they walked away from the pickup the radio got louder to compensate, the repeated phrase following them all the length of the hill.

"Fred is. Fred is dead."

# 10

After Bill left the hall, Janet was kept busy getting the wounded ready to travel. She thought she'd got round to everyone when a well-known voice called out.

"Doctor, I've been waiting for hours here."

Ellen Simmons sat on the far side of the hall. A bandage around her skull was already seeping red, but the obvious blow to the head hadn't made the woman any quieter...or improved her disposition.

"About time too," she said when Janet walked over to check on her. "I would have thought, what with being a patient of long standing, you might have got to me sooner. Especially before *those* people."

*I'm afraid to ask.*

"What people would those be?" Janet said, deliberately keeping her tone neutral. Ellen Simmons wasn't so circumspect. She waved an arm to include most of the folks in front of her in the hall.

"You know very well," she said, loud enough for most of those present to hear her. "Trailer trash. I wouldn't be surprised if they weren't the cause of all this trouble in the first place. I've told the sheriff often enough."

Two men nearby looked ready to take offence, but Janet managed to get them to sit still by giving them a stern look.

"Maybe you should keep your voice down, Ellen," she said. "Passions are running high tonight."

"That's exactly what I'm talking about," the older woman replied, as loud as ever. "Passions are always running high down in the trailers. They're at it like rabbits, all the time. I saw that Fred Grant walking his latest whore just this evening, not long before it all started. What with them and the biker gang it's no surprise the town's in trouble."

*Biker gang? Again, I'm afraid to ask.*

She was saved from having to answer. One of the two men did indeed take offense this time.

"What are you on about, you old bat? Ain't no biker gangs around here. If there were, I'm sure they'd have paid you a visit personally by now."

"Bats. That's what they were," another voice shouted before anyone else could speak. "Giant bats. I saw one of them, clear as day."

"Don't be stupid. Weren't no bats. It was stealth fighters. Goddamned government experiment gone wrong."

Then everyone in the place was shouting. Everything and anything was invoked as the cause of the night's disaster, from witches to demons, *Ruskies* to

UFO, HAARP to FEMA.

Janet stood there, trying to make sense of the chorus of voices, remembering the blue saucer rising up out of Hopman's Hollow.

*What in the blazes is going on here?*

* * *

It took the return of the sheriff to calm things down. It wasn't that he had any new insights on the town's predicament, or any good news to impart, but his physical presence, air of authority and his reputation for taking no nonsense were more than enough to get the respect of everyone present. Even Ellen Simmons fell quiet, for a moment at least.

"We're heading out," he shouted. "All aboard that's going aboard."

People started to shuffle out of the hall.

"All set, Doctor?" Bill said to Janet.

"Ready when you are, Sheriff."

"Well I for one refuse to leave until we're told just who is responsible for this farce."

Janet didn't have to turn round to know who had spoken. Ellen Simmons' voice was unmistakable, especially in such close quarters.

The sheriff took it in stride.

"That's just peachy by me, Ellen. It'll leave more room for somebody who really needs it. The rest of us are getting out of here."

Bill and Janet managed to shepherd everybody out. Janet wasn't surprised to see Ellen Simmons exit alongside everyone else.

People gathered in a growing crowd in the car

park outside the church hall. Apart from the reddish glow in the sky in the north, above where the trailer park had been, there was nothing apart from some bandages on the gathered people to show the severity of what had unfolded scant hours before. Several yellow school buses sat in the parking area outside the hall. The sheriff walked over to the one nearest the road, and Janet followed him over. Two men got out and stood at the door.

"You sober, Charlie?" Bill said. Both Charlie and Fred Grant, who stood beside him, replied.

"Yes, sir."

Both were so obviously trying to appear more sober than they actually were that Janet might have laughed in other circumstances. Charlie straightened up and threw the sheriff a mock salute. Suddenly he looked much more like a man in control of himself.

"Reporting for duty, sir," he said, his tone crisp and military-style. Janet remembered stories she'd heard of Charlie's service in Vietnam, and his long, stoic battle against the wounds he'd received there.

*He might be the right man for the job after all.*

"As long as you're sure?" Bill said.

"Just give the order, sir," Charlie replied, and saluted again.

Bill laughed.

"And you can cut that shit out right now, soldier, or I'll have you peeling potatoes for a month."

Bill turned to Janet.

"Start getting them onboard, Doc," he said. "I'll join you once we get everybody set."

The boarding started. Fred Grant helped Janet get the less able of the wounded up into the bus. There were two other buses in the car park, and a small convoy of pickup trucks and taxis. Alongside the walking wounded, more townspeople arrived every minute. Bill had said they would move out as one. It looked like the town had taken him at his word, and was even now starting to line up in an orderly queue behind his squad car. Charlie and Fred's bus was first in the queue behind that. Janet considered joining Bill in the squad car, but immediately decided against it. Her place was with the wounded, for now at least. She waited until the bus filled up, then stepped up inside.

"Can we go now?" a well-known voice called out. Ellen Simmons was making her presence felt again.

Charlie was in the driver's seat, with Fred Grant at his shoulder. He saluted again as Janet stepped up beside him.

"All aboard that's coming aboard," Charlie said in a singsong voice. "Get your kicks on Route 66."

Janet looked the man in the eye.

"You sure you're sober, Charlie?"

"About as sober as I'm hoping to be," he replied. Fred patted him on the shoulder.

"Don't worry, Doc. He's got enough coffee in him to float a boat, and I'll make sure he stays on the straight and narrow."

That didn't fill her with confidence, given that Fred didn't seem quite sober either. She had been planning to sit with one of the more seriously wounded for the journey, but after seeing the drivers, she decided she'd stay up front, ready to take over if needed.

"Any idea where we're headed?" Charlie asked.

"Town limits to the west first, then on to County Hospital," Janet replied.

"Right you are, Doc. First star to the left, and straight on till morning."

The sheriff led them out minutes later.

* * *

The view from a high position through the front window gave Janet plenty of opportunity to see what was happening to the town. To the left of the road everything looked normal, sturdy and serene. But on the northern side the town had fallen into chaos. There were no collapsed holes as such in the immediate area, but the houses showed evidence of severe subsidence, most of them having fallen in on themselves to various degrees; roofs listing, walls collapsed or, in some cases, fallen in completely.

Janet got another indication of the scale of the disaster as they crested Hope Hill and drove past the church. What had been the neatest cemetery in the county was gone, replaced by a gaping black hole. Tombstones, like gray teeth, lay toppled on the sides of the new chasm, and Janet saw two corpses, obviously torn and tossed from their coffins. The old church itself, a feature in the town since its building almost two hundred years before, had sunk in on one side, giving it a lopsided look. Its northern edge perched precariously over a cliff that hadn't been there an hour before. Several of the passengers on the bus let out wails at the sight, and Janet was grateful as they drove on and left the grisly scene behind.

As they turned onto the approach, to the western outskirts of town, she started to hope they might be free and clear when she noticed that all of the buildings, on both sides of the road, seemed to have escaped any damage. She even stopped worrying about Charlie's driving; he seemed more than capable of keeping the bus in a straight line, which was almost all that would be required for the long stretch of road ahead.

"Don't worry, Doc," Fred said at her side. "The old buzzard knows what he's doing."

"Most fun I've had with my trousers on," Charlie replied, and cackled.

Janet let herself relax slightly. Then she heard it. At first she wasn't sure, as the bus itself was old; the engine far from quiet. But when a fresh nosebleed started, she knew. The hum had returned.

*We're in trouble.*

A child screamed, and the passengers moved restlessly.

"Doc?" someone called out. "We're going to need more cotton swabs back here. I got another nosebleed."

"Me too."

"And me."

Janet tasted blood on her own lip, and saw Charlie wipe fresh blood away from his left nostril onto the arm of his shirt.

"Should have had more JD," he said. But he kept the bus in a straight line, although he now had pain etched in his eyes.

Pressure built. Janet felt tension tighten the muscles of her chest and neck and tried, unsuccessfully, to calm a heart that threatened to thud out of her rib cage. Her head felt like it had been clamped in a vise again, one that was tightening by the second. The child's screams continued, louder and more forceful now, and were joined by other shouts of pain and confusion. Some of the passengers started to get out of their seats, seemingly intent on heading for the door.

"Sit down," Charlie shouted in a voice that surprised her with the force and authority in it. "Sit down, now, or I'll kick your asses from here to Kansas and back."

He didn't take his eyes from the road, but it had worked; whether by shock tactics or sheer force of personality, the passengers returned to their seats. The bus bounced and rocked, as if the road surface itself was moving beneath them.

The hum got louder, and the pressure in Janet's skull grew until she felt she might scream.

The squad car ahead of them lurched violently and almost went off road before getting back on a straight line. The bus bounced, as if the road had suddenly become a switchback. She saw Charlie glance in the side mirror, and then his knuckles whitened as he gripped the wheel tighter.

"Doc," he said, keeping his voice low. "I'd grab hold of something. Things are about to get a mite bumpy."

Janet grabbed the nearest vertical handrail. The bus rocked left, then right. Something in the suspension squealed in protest.

*We'll bust an axle if this keeps up.*

She had to hold tight to avoid being thrown off her feet. A fresh jolt threw her sideways, and as she instinctively gripped the handrail tighter, there was a tug and hot tear at her shoulder that told her she'd done some muscle damage that would hurt like blazes later. Finally she found her balance and got both hands on the rail. The rear end of the bus bounced several feet off the road and came back down with a crash that threw folks from their seats and knocked out the rear window in a tumble of glass and screeching metal. The vehicle swayed sharply left, then right again, before Charlie got it straight.

"We're clear," he shouted.

Janet remembered to breathe. Fred turned and raised a thumb. There was no accompanying smile. His face had gone white, and his expression was grim.

"Those behind us ain't been so lucky."

* * *

Bill brought the squad car to a screeching halt, forcing Charlie to hit the brakes hard and stop the bus just short of running into the other vehicle. The sheriff got out of the squad car and headed back down the road, along the side of the bus and out of Janet's sight. The bus was full of shouting, angry passengers.

"Anybody that wants out is free to go," Charlie said. He hadn't spoken loudly, but his voice seemed to cut through all other conversation, bringing it to an abrupt halt. The bus fell quiet. Ellen Simmons looked fit to burst, but it was obvious to Janet that even the town harridan had been, for now at least, quelled by Charlie's obvious sincerity.

Janet heard Bill call out beyond the rear of the bus, a cry of pain.

"Let me out," she said, pushing past Fred and making for the door.

Charlie opened the door, but put a hand on her arm.

"There ain't nothing you'll want to see, Doc," he said.

"I'm not going to *see* anything, Charlie," she said, so quiet that only he and Fred would hear. "The sheriff needs me."

Charlie nodded, and looked her in the eye.

"Just prepare yourself, Doc. It ain't pretty."

She discovered that for herself seconds later. She stepped down off the bus and joined Bill at the rear.

It was also now the rear of the convoy.

There was no sign of any of the other vehicles that had been following; they were all lost, gone down into a new black pit that stretched from close to their feet off along the road, as far as they could see in the dark. All that remained of the convoy that had followed them was a few wisps of steam rising from the hole, and even that was swiftly dispersed in the breeze.

Bill called out. "Anybody needing help?"

There was no reply, no sound save the chugging of the school bus engine.

Bill started forward. He might have thrown himself down into the hole if Janet hadn't held him back.

"No, Bill. We need you here."

He struggled for several seconds, but not too hard. It was as if most of his fight had drained out of him at the sight of the hole and what had just happened.

"That was near half the townsfolk," Bill whispered. His face went white, and he started to tremble. "Gone like they've never been here." Tears ran down his cheeks.

She took him by the hand.

"We can come back," she said. "Come back and check for survivors once we find someone to help. But we need to get those who are left to safety. And we need to do it fast. We don't know where or when it'll happen again."

Bill wiped absentmindedly at the fresh blood that dripped from his left nostril, leaving a long smear on the arm of his shirt. He looked into the hole one last time; then he let Janet pull him away.

"I'll be back," he whispered, and Janet knew it was a promise, not just to the folks lost in the deep, but to himself.

When Bill headed for the squad car, she went with him, waving to Charlie and Fred on the way past to let them know. She got in the passenger seat.

"Somebody's gonna pay for this," Bill said. He had fresh tears running down both cheeks, leaving clean trails in the night's accumulated grime. But his eyes were bright and clear.

Janet realized something else. The hum had gone again, as fast as it had come. Her nosebleed had stopped and the headache, although not quite gone, had faded into the background.

Bill put the squad car in gear and drove away.

She saw in her wing mirror that the bus fell in behind them. Behind that there was only a yawning darkness.

# 11

They didn't get far.

It was only five minutes after they left the collapse behind when Fred turned to check that their passengers were all okay, just as Charlie hit the brakes again, almost throwing him off his feet.

"What did you go and do that for?" Fred said, then looked out the front window, and saw for himself.

A long barricade of wood and metal blocked the main road out of town. Four guards stood on the other side, and Fred noticed the automatic weapons in their hands before he realized that all four wore cream-colored HAZMAT suits covering them from head to toe, visors closed down to obscure their faces.

Ahead of the bus, the sheriff had stopped the squad car within six feet of the barrier. He got out of the car, and the armed men tensed visibly. One of them raised his weapon. Charlie had his side window rolled down, so they were able to hear the exchange that followed.

"Get back in the car, sir," the guard with the raised weapon said.

"I'm Sheriff Wozniak," Big Bill said. "Who's in charge here?"

"Get back in the car, sir," the guard said again.

The sheriff put his hand on his pistol, and at that all four raised their weapons.

"Get back in the car and turn around, sir, or we'll be forced to shoot you."

Doc got out of the squad car, and that didn't help matters any.

"Get back in the car," the armed guard said, his voice rising to almost a shout. "We have our orders. Nobody gets out."

Doc walked forward, hands raised to show she wasn't armed.

"Stop or I'll shoot," the guard shouted. He sounded as frightened as Fred felt. Doc didn't look to be in any mood to give way.

"We have a busload of wounded and I am a doctor. I demand..."

The guard fired two rounds into the ground at her feet. The sheriff reached for his gun again, and at the same moment the other three trained their weapons on him.

"Don't do it, sir. Please, don't do it."

"Bill," Doc said. "Get back in the car."

"What about our wounded?" the sheriff shouted. "They need help."

"We have our orders. Nobody gets in or out until morning."

"Morning? There won't be anything left of the town by then."

That didn't get a reply. The four guards kept their guns raised.

"For the last time, get back in the car and turn around."

Fred could see that Sheriff Bill was angry, but wasn't stupid enough to do anything rash when faced with four automatic rifles. The big man got back into the squad car, and Doc joined him in the passenger side.

"Best back up, Charlie," Fred said. "Looks like we're heading back to town."

Charlie reversed and did a three-point turn, backing up just far enough to give the sheriff room to pass them on the road. They followed the squad car away from the barricade.

"Where now?" Fred said softly.

Charlie spat out of the window.

"If I know Big Bill, he won't be taking this well. I'd guess we'll be looking for another way out."

Fred wasn't particularly surprised when the sheriff stopped as soon as they were out of view of the guards. Doc and the sheriff got out of the squad car and boarded the bus. They were immediately bombarded with questions, with Ellen Simmons being particularly vocal.

"Why ain't you doing your job, Sheriff? We pay you to look after us, not lie down as soon as a fed points a rifle at you."

"Four rifles, if I counted right," the sheriff said. "And they did a bit more than point them. Trust me, Ellen. These guys ain't diddling around. They'll kill anybody that tries to get through them."

The woman's reply was full of scorn, leaving no one on the bus in any doubt of her views on the matter.

"They cannot stop us. I know my rights. And so should you, Sheriff. We should turn around and ram our way through that barricade. It ain't nothing but some planks of wood."

The sheriff smiled thinly.

"That's twice tonight you've come up with a stupid idea, Ellen. But here's the squad car keys," he said, dangling them in his fingers. "You're welcome to them if you want to try."

The woman looked around, her face telling the story. She expected allies. There were none forthcoming. Fred tried to hide a smile as she sat down and pointedly turned her head away.

The sheriff spoke again, loud enough for everybody to hear.

"It looks like we ain't gonna be allowed to leave town; at least not until sunup. As I see it, we've got several options. We can wait here until morning and have another go at persuading them to let us through, we can go back to town and sit it out, or we can try option three...head for the old forest road and make our way out over the hills."

Fred could see the forest road in his mind; he'd been up there on a skidoo a couple of times in the winter, and as he remembered it, it was going to be a tough haul to get the school bus along that track. But he held his tongue. This was Big Bill's show, his responsibility.

"What do you think is best, Sheriff?" someone

said from the back of the bus.

"I'd like to try the forest road," Big Bill said. "But I know some of you folks are hurting, so I'll go with whatever you decide."

Ellen Simmons once again looked ready to argue, but she didn't speak. To Fred's surprise it was Charlie who voiced what most were thinking.

"I ain't keen on going back to town," the older man said. "All that's there are more holes waiting to eat us up. And who's to say we're any safer sitting here? I'm with Big Bill. I say we head for the hills."

There was an immediate chorus of assent. Fred was looking straight at Ellen Simmons. The woman's mouth was turned down at the corners in disapproval, but she'd learned not to speak up. Fred couldn't help but wonder how long her silence might last if things didn't quite go to plan.

"The squad car ain't gonna make it up the forest road," the sheriff said. "So if it's okay by Charlie, I'll ride with you folks?"

"Fine by me, boss," Charlie said, and threw another mock salute.

While the sheriff transferred his gear from the squad car, Charlie and Fred got some smokes lit. Fred heard the flick of lighters behind him as others followed their cue.

"This is a no-smoking bus," he heard Ellen Simmons say.

"Lady, tonight, I don't give a fuck," someone said, and there was a chorus of laughs in the bus.

A minute later the sheriff returned, Charlie got the bus started and they headed out.

* * *

"You're in charge, Big Bill," Charlie said. There were now four of them at the front of the bus, Doc standing at Bill's shoulder, staring out at the gloom beyond the headlights. "Which way from here?"

Their first hurdle was an obvious one. They had to get past the collapse that had swallowed the convoy.

"Go south past the Bedford farm," the sheriff replied. "We'll be heading well away from any of the collapses we've seen so far. It leads us almost directly onto the old forest track if we cut across the Patersons' paddock. And there's the bonus that it's a quiet road. Maybe the feds ain't got out that way yet and we'll get a clear run at it."

Fred couldn't get the route fixed in his head, but Charlie seemed to know where he was going. They turned off the main highway a minute later and were soon weaving and turning along a network of little more than farm tracks. The bus bounced and rattled across the ruts, but nobody complained of the bumpy ride. Charlie kept the speed low; there were no other lights apart from the bus's own headlights, just enough for them to see twenty yards or so ahead at any given time. They passed a farm that Fred recognized—the Carltons' place. Jed, their youngest, had been in his class in junior high, and they'd spent some time together one summer back then, shooting rabbits in these fields.

"I ain't been out this way since I was a boy," Fred said.

Charlie smiled sadly.

"I started out here myself. And it ain't changed much. Poor folks getting slowly poorer until they wear out and die, leaving more poor folk to take over." He spat out of the window. "Didn't you ever wonder why I signed up for 'Nam?"

The bus bounced along more rutted tracks for ten minutes, and eventually rumblings of discontent started among the passengers. Charlie merely laughed. He clicked on the intercom mike and his voice filled the vehicle.

"Ain't gonna get any smoother, folks. Better get used to it. Or maybe I'll just stop and let those that want to get out?"

They drove on in silence after that.

There was no sign of any fresh ground collapses out here, but neither was there any sign of life. Normally on a night drive in the country, headlights would pick out critters in the road—rabbit, hare, 'coons and, as Fred knew all too well, deer. Fred realized he hadn't seen any wildlife at all since before everything had gone to shit. Not even one of the black crows that were normally so noisily present on the rooftops; though whether they too had been sucked down into the dark, or whether they'd been smart enough to fly off, there was no way of knowing.

They passed three farms in the next ten minutes, but there were no lights on in any of them, and no trucks in the driveways. Fred was trying hard not to think of the people lost when the road under their convoy collapsed. He only hoped that these poor farmers had chosen another way out of town.

The booze he'd had earlier was wearing off now, his thoughts clearing. It wasn't something he was particularly happy about, and he now wished he'd had the foresight to sneak a bottle of bourbon from the bar when they left. Given their current predicament, it might be some time before he tasted liquor again, and he foresaw many nightmares between now and then.

*At least I've got some smokes.*

He lit up two more and passed one to Charlie, who sucked in a deep breath of smoke, none of which seemed to come back out.

The sheriff and Doc had moved back a step, deep in a whispered conversation. Fred leaned in close to Charlie so no one else could hear.

"So what do you think, old man? Is this old bus gonna get us up through the woods?"

Charlie shrugged. "It's gonna have to. I don't see we've got any other options. And we'll find out soon enough."

He pointed out the window. The tree line was only a couple of hundred yards away and they were closing fast.

* * *

"What the hell is that?" Charlie said. Fred had been looking up at the dark silhouette of the hill, and it was only when he lowered his gaze to check the tree line itself that he saw what Charlie meant. The bus headlights picked out a small truck lying on its side, wheels still spinning. Smoke belched from the grate, and something pale waved from a broken window—a bloodstained arm, waving for help.

*Somebody's alive in there.*

Charlie had obviously seen the same thing. He brought the bus to a shuddering stop, hitting the brakes so hard that some of the passengers were thrown from their seats, bringing yells and curses echoing down the bus.

Fred was too busy to bother with that. Surprising even himself, he leapt out as soon as Charlie opened the door. He made straight for the burning truck. He heard more shouts from behind him, but didn't stop. Twin shadows danced ahead of him, thrown long by the bus headlights, darkening his destination so that he didn't spot the holes in the truck until he was almost on top of it.

*Big holes, like the sort made by big guns.*

The pale arm kept waving, and as he closed in he heard someone shouting, a young girl by the sound of it.

"Help me, please."

He circled round to the far side of the truck, hoping to get easier access from the front end, but there was only a tangle of mangled hood and a windshield that wasn't quite busted enough for it to be kicked in. He had to climb up and open the passenger door from above. A girl hung awkwardly in her seat belt. Fred looked at her mop of blonde hair, and his heart lurched.

*Not again. I won't lose another one.*

Looking down he saw two bodies below the girl—an older couple, most probably her parents. The older woman had a broken neck, while the man's cause of death was all too apparent. He had a penny-size bullet hole in his forehead from which blood still dripped.

*What happened here?*

The girl moaned, and turned to look up. She looked Fred in the eye and when she spoke, blood bubbled at her lips.

"Help me, please."

"Just hold on," Fred said. "We'll have you out of there in no time."

It proved to be harder than he would have hoped. He tried to get her out of the belt, but her whole weight was on it, pulling at the buckle and stopping it from disengaging. No matter from which direction he tugged, he couldn't get her free.

"I need some help here," he shouted, and at the same moment felt a hand on his shoulder. The sheriff climbed up alongside him. The big man looked down into the truck and sucked air through his teeth.

"Somebody's going to pay for this night," he muttered, then turned to Fred.

"Get down inside," he said. "You should be able to squeeze down to get under her and lift her weight off the belt."

Fred started to drop himself, feet first, through the window. The girl moaned, then yelped in pain as he squeezed past her. His feet landed on something soft.

*I'm standing on her mother.*

He pushed the thought away and forced his attention on to the job at hand.

It took some contortions by Fred and some heavy lifting from the sheriff, but they managed to get the girl out of the truck, and Fred was more than happy to climb out after her. He didn't look down, even when his footing gave way and slid from under him. He grabbed the lip of the window and hauled himself up, taking in huge gasps of air that tasted as sweet as a hit of sugar. He helped the sheriff take the girl's weight and they were in the process of lowering her to the ground when a shout came from behind them.

"Get back in the bus, please. Turn around and go back to town."

Fred had heard that tone already, back at the barricade. He knew what he was going to see even before he turned.

A row of men in hazard suits walked out of the forest. They were spaced ten yards apart and the line stretched off into the dark for as far as Fred could see. All carried automatic rifles, and the nearest had his weapon pointed straight at them.

"This girl needs hospital treatment," the sheriff said.

"Get back in the bus, please. Turn around and go back to town."

"Change the record," Big Bill said. "Can't you see she needs help…"

His pleadings were cut short by a short burst of automatic fire. Dirt and pebbles flew from the ground at their feet.

"Get back in the bus, please. Turn around and go back to town."

Even then Bill looked like he was going to make a stand, until the girl in their arms moaned, coughed and expelled a mouthful of blood.

"Maybe Doc…" Fred said, trying not to stare at the man holding the weapon on them.

Big Bill spat at his feet.

"Maybe," he said. The sheriff took the girl's

weight, lifted her in his arms and without another word turned back to the bus. Fred had one last try.

"We just want to get to safety," he said.

"Get back in the bus, please. Turn around and..."

Fred raised a hand and turned away.

"I know...go back to town. Do us a favor, would you? Come and look for us in the morning...if there's any of us left."

He followed the sheriff back to the bus.

# 12

Bill and Fred carried the girl onto the bus and laid her out on the floor beside Charlie. Passengers stood and gathered round until Bill moved them away. Janet pushed her way through.

"Give Doc some space," he said. "This girl needs treatment, and she needs it now."

As ever, the sheriff's tone was enough to get them all back into their seats, but there was a new buzz of conversation around her as Janet knelt at the stricken girl's side.

"Where does it hurt?" she asked.

The girl tried to speak. Fresh blood bubbled at her lips and Janet was kept busy for the next few minutes trying to assess the damage. The girl was in distress at first, but calmed somewhat as the tranquilizer that Janet administered started to take effect.

The girl only spoke once, just as she was going under the influence of the drug, and it didn't make much sense to Janet.

"Watch out for the bears."

Then she went under, her breathing finally slowing and heart rate coming down enough that Janet felt safe in doing a full examination. At first she was worried the girl might have internal injuries, but the blood in her mouth proved to be from where she'd bitten into her tongue. She also had deep bruises from where the seat belt had grabbed at her shoulder and a graze on her knee that had taken the skin off almost to the bone. But Janet was finally able to sit back on her heels and look up at Bill.

"She'll live," she said.

"Well, for the same time as the rest of us anyway," Bill replied, grimly. "Although I ain't too sure it's going to be for long."

Janet knew that Charlie had turned the bus around and driven away from the woods, but after that she'd been busy with the girl.

"Where are we headed?"

Bill looked tired and worn.

"We're thinking maybe The Roadside. It's on the far edge of town from the collapses, at least the ones we've seen so far. It's either that or just stop where we are and wait it out, but folks will need toilet trips, and water, and..."

She put a hand on his arm.

"The Roadside sounds like a good plan to be getting on with. Once we get there we can regroup, come up with a strategy. It's only a couple of hours until morning."

The rest of the passengers looked shell-shocked and resigned—apart from one. Ellen Simmons stared at Janet with something that looked like pure venom.

*I wonder what slight I've given her now?*

Whatever Ellen Simmons' problem was, it was minor in the current scheme of things. She checked on her other patients, making sure most were at least comfortable, and when she next looked up, Charlie was bringing the bus into The Roadside car park.

* * *

Janet spent the next five minutes making sure everybody got off the bus safely before recruiting Fred's help with the girl. The youth was only too happy to oblige, taking most of the weight as they walked across the short stretch of parking lot and into the bar. They got her into one of the padded seats against the wall. She was still out cold, but started to stir as they stood back, carefully, each waiting to move quickly if she showed any sign of either falling off the seat, or waking in a confused state.

Most of the patients were subdued and quiet, cowed by what the night had brought upon them, but it didn't take Ellen Simmons long to make her presence felt once everyone was gathered in the main bar area.

"I never thought I'd see the day when we had a coward for a sheriff," she said, loudly so that everyone was sure to hear. She stood in the center of the bar, hands on hips. "I'd be thoroughly ashamed of myself if I was you, Bill Wozniak."

"I could say the same right back at you," Bill said sharply, then shook his head and raised a hand. "No, sorry, I didn't mean that. We're all tired and..."

Ellen Simmons barked a laugh.

"See. You ain't even able to insult me properly. We need strength and leadership here, not somebody turned into a moon-eyed boy by the charms of a Jezebel."

*Charms of a Jezebel?* Janet thought. *I rather like that.*

Bill went red at that, his fists clenched. He strode forward towards the older woman, and for a second Janet thought he might hit her. Instead he stopped six feet from her, and took a deep breath, looking for calm before replying.

"And what would you have had me do, Ellen?" Bill said. He spoke softly, but everyone in the room heard him.

"Your job," the woman said. By now she was almost shouting. "You should have got us to safety. That's what we pay you for."

Janet's mouth ran ahead of her thinking, and she spoke up when it was obvious that Bill wouldn't rise to the bait.

"And I suppose you'd be happy if we all got killed in the process?"

"Pah," the woman said. "They wouldn't have killed us."

A small voice spoke up.

"They done killed my ma and pa."

The bar fell quiet, and everyone turned to look. The girl was awake. She looked pale, almost gray, but she sat up straight in her seat, and Janet was pleased to see that the flow of blood from the injured tongue had stopped and that the wound wasn't bad enough to stop the girl from talking.

"Shot Pa in the head," the girl said. Janet moved towards her, but Fred Grant beat her to it. He sat down beside the girl and put an arm around her shoulders. She didn't protest.

"You don't have to talk about it," he said softly.

She shook her head, and looked determined.

"That old bat don't know what she's talking about," the girl said. Janet was watching Ellen Simmons, and had to hide a grin at the look that crossed the older woman's face as the girl continued. "They done shot Pa, and all he did was try to drive up the track. Ma's dead too, I guess, if she ain't here."

Everybody in the room went quiet at that. The only noise was the soft sound of pouring liquid as Charlie helped himself to a beer. Janet realized for the first time that she knew the girl; Sarah Bennett, a quiet girl of nineteen or so who normally sat in the waiting room while her mother, Agnes, got her weekly diabetes checkup. She'd never heard the girl speak before now. But now that's she'd started, Sarah was in no mood to stop.

"Pa weren't in no mood to take any shit," she said. "Not after the barns got ate up by the holes and the bears started to growl. We got out of the farm like lickety-spit and headed for Aunt Ellie's over the hill. She's waiting for us. She'll be so worried..."

Her eyes widened and her eyelids fluttered. Afraid that the girl might faint, Janet was on the move, but before she could reach them, the girl started to sob. Fred Grant tightened his grip on her shoulders. She leaned her head against his chest, then seemed to gather some resolve to speak again and looked up.

"Pa was never one for obeying the feds," she said softly. "And he weren't about to start now. So when they stopped us at the forest track, he cursed them, long and hard. Ain't hardly ever heard Pa use language like that when he hadn't had a drink, but by then he was as angry as a bag of squirrels. The men with the guns told us to turn around and go back to town, and then Pa told *them* where to go, and tried to drive through. They shot him in the head. He was driving, and they shot him in the head. We hit a stone at the side of the track and..."

She didn't have to say any more. Everyone present had seen the truck on its side, and could imagine how it got that way. The girl pressed her face against Fred Grant's chest and started to sob again. He patted her hair awkwardly and looked more than a little embarrassed. But he didn't draw away, holding the girl until her sobbing subsided into a muffled sniffle.

Even Ellen Simmons had the good grace not to fill the silence with her rancor.

Once it was clear that the girl was done talking, Janet turned to Big Bill.

"Who are they? The men in the suits?"

Bill shrugged.

"Feds? FEMA? Or maybe the CDC?"

That gave Janet pause for thought. If it were the CDC, it would explain the extreme measures being taken to contain the townsfolk.

"They think it's an outbreak?" she said. She tried to keep her voice low, but Ellen Simmons heard her.

"An outbreak? Like in that film?" the older woman shouted. "Well that settles it. I'm not waiting here for the government to kill me off or for some filthy foreign disease to eat me up." She looked to Big Bill again. "I demand that we get out of here. Right now."

Big Bill walked over to her and put the squad car

keys in her hand.

"There you go, Ellen. You know where I left it. Good luck."

The sheriff turned back to Janet, leaving the Simmons woman to splutter behind him.

"Let's say it is an outbreak," he said. "What happens next?"

She thought back to everything she'd read in the sporadic bulletins the government medical officers sent out to town doctors. It wasn't much, but Janet knew there were strict procedures in place for such eventualities. She just never expected to be on the receiving end of them. Bill was still waiting for a reply.

"After containment, they'll start to come into town to take samples," she said. "Probably not before sunup, when they can get a clearer picture of the extent of...whatever this thing is."

Bill nodded.

"About what I thought. Let's take inventory and squat down here. At least until we know what's what."

Another thought struck Janet.

"Bears," she said. Bill looked at her quizzically, as if she'd suddenly gone mad.

*And maybe I have.*

"Sarah said there were bears. My guess is for her it's bears. For you it's devils, for me it's little gray men. Too much X-Files, I guess."

Fred Grant looked up at that.

"And for me it's ghosts."

"I see where you're heading with this," Bill said. "We're all projecting our own fears, is that it?"

"Something like that. If the CDC is here, it could

be a chemical agent, acting on our brains."

She'd momentarily forgotten that others were listening. Within seconds the room was full of animated conversation, those who were able to relating all of the weird shit they had seen at the time of the collapses.

*"I done told you already, it were black helicopters."*

*"No…Ruskies. I saw them, clear as day."*

*"Weren't no Ruskies. Not unless Ruskies can grow fangs and make their eyes glow in the dark."*

It seemed Janet was indeed onto something. Each person that had seen something had experienced it in a different way from anyone else.

*But there's something else.*

It was Bill who voiced what was starting to worry her.

"I'll tell you something for nothing. There's more going on here than the CDC knows about. Those holes aren't in our heads. Neither were the bodies we found at the Hopman place. And another thing… Doc and I both saw that…*saucer*…come up out of the ground."

Fred spoke up.

"And I wasn't the only one who felt the *ghosts* or saw things move around. Whatever is going on here, it's communal. Did you ever hear about anything like that, Doc?"

And just like that, Janet felt fear grip at her, hard, a cold chill on her spine she couldn't shake.

"No sense in speculating," she said. "If it is the CDC, they'll be here soon enough, and we'll see what we'll see. For now, just keep warm. And stay alert."

The only way to keep her mind from racing was

to work. She busied herself tending to the wounded, making sure everybody was comfortable. She was relieved to find that everyone seemed more or less stable, although many were weak and wan.

"Bill," she said. "We need to get some hot food and drink inside folks."

"That's our first priority," he agreed. He looked over at the bar. "Charlie. Put that beer down and get into the kitchen. See if we can rustle up some field rations?"

Once again the older man threw the sheriff a mock salute. He didn't put the beer down, but he carried it with him as he headed for the kitchen. Fred Grant moved to join him, but Sarah Bennett wasn't having any of that. She held tight to Fred's arm, pulling him back into the seat.

"Don't leave me," she said. She looked like the thought of being left alone was enough to have her quivering with fear. Fred sat back in his seat, and the girl snuggled up against him, as if his presence alone calmed her. Once again Fred looked more than slightly embarrassed.

Janet smiled.

"Stay put, Fred, I'll give Charlie a hand in the kitchen."

"Check out the cold store and pantry for provisions," Bill said. "I'll be back in a minute."

"Where are you going?" Janet said, surprised to hear panic rising in her voice. It wasn't just the new girl who needed the comfort of having someone she trusted stay close by.

Bill pulled her into a hug.

"Don't worry. I'm just going to check the situation

outside. I want to be sure we're safe before we set up what might be a permanent camp."

He gave her a peck on the cheek and left. Janet immediately felt a twinge of fear and uncertainty. She pushed it down.

*He's the sheriff. He can take care of himself.*

She also knew that the only way she'd be able to stop worrying was to do something, anything, while Bill was away. She turned from the door. Ellen Simmons smirked at her as she made her way to the kitchen.

*We're going to have more trouble from that one.*

* * *

But all thoughts of Ellen Simmons were completely forgotten when she entered the kitchen. The room was dark, black shadows creeping in the corners. It felt cold, clammy almost.

"Charlie?" She had meant to shout, but somehow all that came out was a strangled sound, hardly more than a whisper. "We haven't got time for silly games."

In reply, the sound of metal scraping on metal came from farther inside the room.

Janet walked past the serving area to the kitchen proper. Charlie was there. He was on his knees, hands clasped behind his head, cowering, as if afraid of an impending beating. Three shadowy figures stood over him. The only light came from the bar behind her so Janet wasn't able to see too clearly, but it was obvious that whoever these men were, they weren't wearing HAZMAT suits. It was equally obvious that they weren't here to help. They all carried rifles, all three of which were pointed at Charlie's head.

Janet didn't think consciously about her next actions. She fumbled for several seconds at the wall before her fingers found what she was looking for. She hit the light switch, at the same time sweeping up a skillet from the nearest work surface. She threw it at the closest attacker, screamed at the top of her voice and threw herself forward. She was still moving, heading for Charlie, when the pan hit its target. The man, if that was what he had ever been, fell apart like a burst bubble. The other two attackers also collapsed, first at knees, then at hips, and by the time Janet got to Charlie, he lay in the center of a spreading pool of *gloop*. The skillet clattered loudly against a cabinet and thrummed for a second before lying still. The only sound was Charlie's stifled sobs, quickly followed by heavy footsteps and alarmed voices from the bar behind them.

A quick check showed that Charlie appeared to be unharmed, but he was still sobbing, quietly, holding it in like a child frightened to make a noise. He looked up at Janet, eyes red and snot dripping from his nose.

"Don't let anybody see me like this," Charlie said. "Please, Doc?" He grabbed her arm and held tight. "Please, Doc?" he said again, little more than a whisper.

"I've got your back, old man," she replied.

She shouted out, just as the kitchen door opened and Fred Grant burst inside.

"I've got it," Janet said, keeping herself in front of Charlie so Fred couldn't see him. "It's just a kitchen accident. We dropped a couple of pans."

Fred stood in the doorway. She saw the confusion on his face.

"Is Charlie okay?" the youth asked.

Janet forced herself to smile, and kept her voice steady despite every nerve in her body screaming at her to run.

"He's fine. Too much excitement for one night, that's all. I'll give him a hand in here for a while. You go back and sit with the girl. She needs the company."

"If you're sure?"

She nodded, and Fred left them, none too reluctantly. When Janet turned back, she found Charlie staring at the mess on the floor around him.

"What the hell is this shit?" he said.

"What's left of whatever attacked you," Janet replied, aware even as she spoke how far into the *Twilight Zone* they had descended.

*These were no thought forms. Whatever is going on, it's definitely physical. And just as definitely weird as all hell.*

The older man didn't seem to be able to process the information she'd given him. He stood, staring at his feet, his fingers fumbling with a battered cigarette packet, trying to get a smoke.

"Here, let me," she said.

She took the packet from him, took out a cigarette and passed it back to him. Even then she had to help him hold his hand steady to use the lighter. He sucked in the first gasp as if his life depended on it. When he looked back at Janet, confusion was written all over his features.

"They were Vietcong," Charlie said. "I'd know those bastards anywhere. But what where they doing here? And where did they go?"

She had no real answer. She looked at the floor, then up at the too-bright lights above. She remembered Bill's *devils* had similarly fallen apart…in the sunshine, in the light. An idea started to form.

"Just keep the lights on," she said.

Charlie looked even more puzzled, but he seemed to have regained some composure, and when he raised the cigarette to his lips, his hands had stopped shaking.

"Light's ain't gonna keep the VC away, Doc," he said. "At least it never worked back in the day." But she saw that he was already wondering whether it had all been in his mind.

"They were never really here," she said. "At least, not in the sense you think."

"They were real enough," he replied. "I ain't had enough to drink to be having the DTs, Doc, if that's what you're thinking?"

She took the old man's free hand and squeezed.

"If it's the DTs, then I'm getting them too," she replied. "No, it's what we said earlier, Charlie. There's something in town playing tricks on us. I don't think it can actually hurt us."

*But don't quote me on that one.*

Charlie looked ready to argue, but thought better of it and went back to sucking down as much smoke as he could get into him. He finally dropped the butt into the nearest sink and turned on the tap, quenching it with a hiss.

He looked at the *gloop* on the floor, and muttered something under his breath that Janet didn't catch—something about old man Hopman and the mineshafts that made little sense to her. He turned and looked Janet in the eye.

"You watch out for me, and I'll watch out for you, Doc. We got a deal?"

She shook on it, and they went to work.

Charlie got three big pots of coffee going while Janet cleared up the mess on the floor. It had already started to rot and stink and took a lot of elbow grease and disinfectant before she was happy it was all gone. It was only after she washed her hands, scrubbing over and over again until her palms felt raw, that she wondered whether she should have taken samples for the CDC.

* * *

She was back in the main bar handing out coffee five minutes later when Big Bill returned. She offered him a cup, but he went straight behind the bar and poured himself three fingers of rye, knocking it back in one gulp before speaking.

"I don't want anybody going outside. Nobody leaves. Got it?"

Janet was watching the sheriff closely. His color was high on his cheeks, and he breathed heavily, as if he'd just been running. He refused to meet anyone's gaze, and the slightest sound had him reaching for his pistol.

*He's spooked. He's seen something.*

Nobody spoke. The sight of the big sheriff in a funk raised the tension in the room noticeably. To Janet's surprise it was Charlie who knew what was needed.

"Hey, Big Bill," the older man said. "If you ain't gonna pay for that booze, I hope you've got enough for all of us?"

A couple of people laughed at that, and the sheriff looked ruefully at the empty glass in his hand.

"I don't see no barman, do you?" he said. "We can settle up with Tony later."

Janet doubted that. She'd seen the barman earlier...getting into one of the other buses; one of those lost when the convoy fell into the collapsed road. She didn't say anything. Charlie had handled the situation deftly enough and the tension, if not gone, had been defused for the moment.

Charlie lightened the mood further by going round behind the bar.

"You heard Big Bill," he said, loud enough for all to hear. "We can settle up later. Form an orderly queue."

Within seconds he had several customers, although Janet was amused to see that Fred Grant wasn't one of them. Sarah Bennett slept with her head on his shoulder, and he stroked her blonde hair, gently, lost in some faraway thought.

Janet passed out the last mug of coffee, and motioned for Bill to meet her in the kitchen. Almost as soon as the door was shut behind them he grabbed her in a bear hug, squeezing so hard she became short of breath.

"Easy, big guy," she said in his ear. "I might be needing these ribs sometime."

His grip eased, slowly. When she pulled her head away and looked him in the eye, he had fresh tears rolling down his cheeks.

"It's that bad?" she whispered.

He nodded.

"The town's not going to be recovering from this. Ain't nobody here but those we have in the bar as far as I can tell. Newman's store has fallen in, as has the bank. Your surgery is still there, but there's a new hole between here and there. And my office is just gone, fallen into some black deep."

He paused as if unsure how to continue.

"You ain't gonna believe me, Janet. But I saw them again, down in the holes. Only they're not holes. They're doorways to hell. And there are devils down there."

She returned his embrace and gave him a soft kiss on the lips.

"You'd be surprised what I'm prepared to believe tonight," she said. She stayed in his arms as she told him what had happened with Charlie and the resulting mess of protoplasm. Some of the sheriff's composure was coming back, slowly but surely, but he showed no signs of letting her go.

"More of that stuff we found when the...*devils*... burned up?"

She nodded.

"I suspect the *stuff* is the cause of what's happening here. Though the *how* of it completely escapes me. And whether it's the cause of, or caused by, the collapsing ground, I have no idea."

"Let's hope we're given enough time to find out," Bill said. "Ain't no way to live, wondering if the ground is going to swallow you up and send you to hell at any second."

They stayed there, holding each other, until a

shout came from the bar beyond.

"Best get through here, Sheriff."

# 13

Several things surprised Fred Grant. He had a girl sleeping on his shoulder, he was sober, and free booze was on offer.

*And I don't want any.*

Despite his drinking from the evening before, the time since then had left him stone-cold sober. The events themselves were already taking on a distant, dreamlike quality. But the girl with her head on his shoulder was real. He had got her out of the truck. Maybe he hadn't saved her life, but he felt responsible for her, in a way that excited and frightened him in equal measure. Maybe it was the blonde hair, and the memory of another girl falling into darkness, or maybe it was just a simple need for contact with another person in troubling times. Whatever it was, he was content, for the moment at least, to sit and let her sleep.

He felt her heat against his arm, like sitting too close to a radiator, but not nearly as uncomfortable. But it brought a memory of another hot body pressed against his legs, and of a glass, spinning, in a cold room, and of words, picked out on the board.

*F...R...E...D...I...S...D...E...A...D*

He came awake with a start as his head nodded to fall on his chest.

*Ain't no sense in sleeping if that's what my dreams are going to be like.*

He stroked the girl's hair again, that simple act bringing him more calm than he'd felt since heaving Charlie out of the hole the morning before. He was almost content.

One person in the room wasn't content at all. Ellen Simmons, taking advantage of the fact that Doc and the sheriff were in the kitchen, tried to take charge.

"We can't just sit here and wait to die," she said.

Fred had some sympathy with that statement. They were caught between a rock and a hard place, but at least here they were warm, and had food and light, as long as they lasted. But the Simmons woman wasn't content with that.

"We've been paying that sheriff for years, for what? To sit on his ass and eat donuts? And now when we need him, where is he? Canoodling with that so-called doctor, that's what. Well I for one am not waiting any longer for him to get a backbone. I'm heading out."

She dangled the squad car keys in her fingers.

"I'm heading for the car, and then to find a way to safety. Who's with me?"

Much to Fred's surprise several of the wounded

stood up, three of them, three more than he had expected. They moved to join Ellen Simmons as she headed for the door.

"We can fit a couple more in, at a squeeze," she said, hand on the door handle.

Nobody took her up on it.

"I'll head for the county sheriff," she said. "I *know* he's got more backbone than Bill Wozniak. He'll be here with help in no time. Just you wait and see."

She pushed the door open, starting to head out.

"I wouldn't do that. There ain't nowhere to go, Ellen," Charlie said from behind the bar. "Nowhere safe, no how."

"And why would I listen to you, Charlie Watson? You've been drunk so long you don't know up from down."

Charlie raised a beer glass and smiled.

"Ain't no skin off my nose, darling," he said. "Just don't let your wounded pride get you killed. Don't let it get these other folks killed."

She sniffed at him as if he were a piece of bad meat, and turned back to the open door.

"We'll be back with help before you know it," she said. "I promise."

"We'll be here," Charlie replied.

The door closed behind the four as they left.

"Best get through here, Sheriff," Charlie shouted.

* * *

Charlie's shout woke the girl up with a start. She made to pull herself away, then seemed to realize where she was and kept her head on Fred's shoulder.

She maintained a strong grip on his arm.

*Don't look like she's aiming to give me up anytime soon.*

He found he wasn't displeased at the idea, but when the sheriff came back into the bar from the kitchen, Fred stood up, ready to help if needed. The girl stood too, still holding on to his arm for dear life.

"What happened?" the Sheriff asked, looking around the bar area.

Charlie waved towards the door.

"Ellen Simmons took off," he said. "Her and three others. Said she was headed for your car, then points west."

For a second Fred thought that the sheriff might just shrug and let it lie, but he saw the squeeze on the arm that Doc gave him.

"You've got to stop her, Bill. I know she's a pain in the ass...but she's one of us. Part of our town. We need to save what we can."

Fred, with Sarah attached, joined Doc and the sheriff as they headed for the door. The sheriff got there first, opened the door wide and yelled out.

"Ellen. Get your stupid butt back here."

Doc laughed.

"Not exactly what I would have said. But at least if she's within hearing distance, she won't be able to stop herself from answering back."

There was no reply. Fred stood behind the sheriff, trying to see past him. All he could see was the small patch of ground lit from the lights inside the bar. Beyond there was only dense blackness. Although they'd only left a matter of seconds before, there was no sign of the party of four.

Bill turned away.

"She's determined. I'll give her that."

"Ellen!" Doc shouted, to no avail. Bill took Doc's arm.

"I doubt she'll make it as far as the squad car. They'll get spooked by the dark and run back here. Any second now."

"Here they come," Sarah said softly.

Something moved in the dark, and Fred suddenly felt in need of a drink as it came forward into view.

It was big, red and seemed to be on fire. Half as big again as a man, and standing on two legs, a *demon* walked out of the dark. It stopped just at the edge of where the light fell on the parking spots outside. Muscles bunched under tight skin, and when it smiled, it showed twin rows of sharp teeth like a shark.

Big Bill tensed, and drew his pistol.

"Stop or I'll shoot."

The demon stopped, head tilted, as if confused by this new sound. It showed no sign of either coming forward, or retreating, just stood there. It was hard to tell in the gloom, but Fred got the distinct impression it was smiling.

"They're learning," Doc whispered. Fred had no idea what that meant, but it didn't sound good.

*Not good at all.*

Doc turned to speak to Fred directly.

"Do you know where the external light switch is? The one for the car park floods?"

Fred nodded. He only had to move three feet to the side of the door, but Sarah moved with him, still gripping tightly to his arm. He used his free hand to flick the switch. Light blazed outside, the demon finally fully visible. It was strangely unformed, smooth and wrinkle free; a bland, featureless face save for two buttonhole eyes and the toothy smile. Even that faded as the light hit it. It melted and ran like a knob of butter on a hot skillet. It backed away almost immediately, sloughing off bubbling flesh, and lumbered off into the darkness, leaving a trail of glistening slime behind it.

Fred reached for the light switch.

"No," Doc said. "Leave it on. It may be the only protection we have."

*She knows more than she's letting on.*

Fred was about to ask more, but Doc put a finger to her lips.

"Later," she mouthed.

Fred saw why when he turned back to the bar. Everybody else was staring at them, quizzical looks on their faces.

*They didn't see it. Big Bill blocked their view.*

Charlie obviously was another who knew more than he was letting on. The older man poured a beer and as Fred went back to his seat, he came round the bar and handed it over.

"Trust me, son, you'll want it."

Fred wasn't about to argue. The rest of the survivors started throwing questions at Big Bill and Doc, leaving Fred with his beer…and Sarah. She didn't say a word, just grabbed his arm tight, put her head on his shoulder, and went back to sleep.

Part of Fred wanted to do the same, just close his eyes and succumb to oblivion for a while and *hope* the dreams stayed away. But the sight of the demon refused to leave him alone and he remained resolutely awake. It felt like a year since he'd woken the previous day, before his life had been turned upside down and inside out.

* * *

By the time he'd had a smoke and finished most of the beer, many of the survivors had, like Sarah, fallen into fitful sleep. Charlie was one of the few still awake. He still sat at the bar, sipping another in an unending line of beers, but the older man seemed to be clear-eyed and remarkably sober—alert even, as if on edge. Looking at him now, Fred could see the young soldier he once had been, not the town drunk who did the jobs no one else wanted to do. More than that, Fred caught a glimpse of what might be waiting for himself in the future; a lonely man in a bar, on the watch for monsters.

*Because there will always be monsters.*

Like Fred, Doc and the sheriff looked determined to stay awake. While Fred sipped the last of his beer they spoke, heads close, whispering, in an exchange that became heated before the sheriff broke off and walked over to stand above Fred.

"Doc says I can trust you," the big man said. "I ain't so sure, but I need some help."

That looked to be as close as the sheriff was going to get to pleading. Fred tried to stand, but Sarah kept him down in his seat until he gently moved her away. She grabbed at his hand as he rose, and clutched it, hard.

"I got somebody to look after now," Fred said to

the sheriff. "But as long as it don't put her back into more danger than we're in already, I'm your man."

The sheriff smiled and looked like a completely different man, as if a weight had just lifted. He took Fred's free hand and shook it.

"I guess you've just been deputized, son. Welcome to law enforcement."

Fred wondered just what he'd let himself in for. The Sheriff must have seen it in his face, and laughed softly.

"Don't worry, lad. I'm not sending anyone out into the night. I just need somebody to stand by the back door and keep watch."

One thought came immediately.

"There ain't no floodlights out back," he said, dismayed to hear the tremor that crept into his voice. "What if that—thing—comes back?"

Doc was now at the sheriff's side.

"Keep the kitchen lights on at all times," she said. "And I'll have a look and see if there's a flashlight around here somewhere."

"The sun will be up before too long," the sheriff added. "And then maybe we can find out exactly what's going on here—and maybe even get some sleep."

*I wouldn't bet on it.*

Charlie gave Fred a smile and a mock salute as they made their way to the kitchen. Sarah went with him, her grip on his hand never loosening.

* * *

He opened the back door slowly. There was some

light beyond it, and he was happy to see a lit bulb immediately above the door on the outside. It didn't light up much beyond a couple of yards of the backyard, but it was enough to ease his mind somewhat about having to stand in darkness.

He immediately regretted ever leaving the warm seat in the bar, but when Sarah leaned into him and put her head on his chest, the booze was quickly forgotten. He lit a cigarette and stared out into the blackness, trying not to let his imagination run wild, trying not to remember everything else that had happened in recent hours.

There was a row of trees out there somewhere—he knew that, but it was still so dark that they couldn't be seen apart from their making a darker shadow just at the edge of his vision. Here at the rear of the kitchen he couldn't hear any sound from the bar, and there was no noise out in the darkness. Once again he was struck by the absence of bird sound, and it had been hours since he'd heard a dog bark. A cloak of silence had fallen over the town, and all he heard was Sarah's soft breathing and the hiss of burning ash at the end of his smoke as he inhaled.

The quiet seeped into him, and he even began to relax—only to almost jump out of his skin when he felt a hand on his shoulder. He let out a small yelp when he turned to see someone behind him.

"It's only me," Doc said. "I found you a flashlight."

Sarah surprised him by reaching out and taking the flashlight from Doc, immediately spraying the beam around the backyard. It lit up a row of garbage bins, a stack of empty beer barrels and a rusted, wheel-less pickup, raised up on bricks. There was no sign of any movement. Sarah seemed happy with that, switched off the flashlight, and once again lowered her head to Fred's chest.

"You've got a new friend," Doc said.

Fred smiled.

"It would seem so," he said. "And I intend to do right by her. You can tell Big Bill I said that."

It was Doc's turn to smile back.

"You've surprised him enough for one night, I think."

All three of them stood together for a while, looking out into the darkness.

"So, fess up, Doc," Fred said as he ground out his smoke on the doorjamb and flicked the butt out into the night. "What do you know?"

She took a while to reply.

"I don't really *know* anything. I have suspicions though..."

"Isn't it time you shared them?"

She looked tired, and maybe even a little afraid.

"I'm not sure that sharing will do anyone any good. But I suppose you have a right to know."

She told him about the *demons* they'd encountered at Hopman's Hollow, and the protoplasm that was left behind.

"It wasn't anything I recognized. There's nothing in my training or reading that leads me to believe that such a thing is even possible."

Fred was thinking again about the glass spinning like a top above the Ouija board as Doc continued.

"It may be that we're here at the birth of a completely new species."

Fred remembered something from an earlier conversation with Charlie.

"Toxic chemicals can cause mutations, can't they? If I'm remembering my schooling right?"

Doc nodded. "In some cases."

He told her Charlie's story, about what he'd seen and what they'd dumped in the mines. Doc went pale.

"That's something the CDC needs to know. And fast."

"I might be misrepresenting Charlie," Fred said. "And you know how he is...it might be just another story but..."

Janet nodded.

"It's a big enough *but* for us to take heed of it. I'll go and talk to him."

She gave his shoulder a squeeze in gratitude, and left.

Almost as soon as Doc had gone, Sarah switched on the flashlight again and made another sweep of the backyard. She stopped at the rusting hulk of the pickup and moved the beam quickly along the length of the vehicle and back again. The dancing shadows gave it the impression of movement.

"Did you see something?" Fred whispered.

"Just the bears," she sobbed, switched off the light and buried her face in his chest.

* * *

They stayed that way for a while. Fred had another smoke, and Sarah's breathing calmed—so much so that he thought she must have fallen back into sleep.

He was surprised when the flashlight came back on. This time she had it trained straightaway on the rusted pickup truck.

"There's something there," she whispered. "In the passenger seat."

Her hand shook so much that the beam of light bobbed alarmingly over the vehicle, once again giving the semblance of movement. Fred reached to take the flashlight from her hand. And at the same instant the shadows inside the truck moved. Legs swung out of the passenger side, and as the beam moved, it showed the rest of the body climbing out of the vehicle.

An old man wearing gray overalls coated in dust and grime stepped out the truck. He carried a pick-axe and wore a hard hat with a broken lamp at the front. Fred grabbed at the edge of the door, ready to slam it shut.

But the figure showed no sign of moving towards them. Fred waved the light on it. Where the beam hit it, the body seemed to waver, almost melt before hardening back into some kind of solidity.

*Damn thing is hardly there at all.*

Sarah had her face buried in his chest again, and he felt the tension grip her.

"Stay back," Fred shouted.

"Fred is dead," the miner replied, the phrase echoing in the backyard until it seemed to come from a chorus of voices. "Fred is dead."

Two seconds later Fred and Sarah were in the kitchen having slammed the door shut. They stood there, breathing heavily, just staring at each other until Fred's heart stopped thudding in his ears and his breathing slowed to something approaching normal.

He listened for a long time, but there was no further sound from outside.

# 14

Janet was still arguing with the sheriff when the sun came up.

"I'm telling you," she said. "The CDC needs to hear this. If what Charlie says is true, then the mines *must* be the source of what is going on here."

"And I'm telling *you*," Bill replied. "I'm not letting anyone else run around out there. Ellen Simmons ain't come back, and I doubt we'll see her anytime soon. Or will you argue with me on that score too?"

They stood in the doorway of The Roadside. The parking lot lights still blazed, but as the sky lightened so too did their impact lessen. That had Janet worried, but there was no sign of any further *attacks*. She was about to remonstrate with Bill when a car alarm sounded somewhere to their left, followed by the telltale buzz in her ears and at her jaw.

The hum had returned.

"Get everybody ready," the sheriff said, wiping

a drop of blood from his nostril onto his sleeve. "We might have to move out fast."

A tree fell over a hundred yards away along the road, then another slightly closer. The car alarm cut off abruptly and a puff of smoke and dust rose in the air from that direction. The hum dissipated, the vibration faded, and everything went suddenly quiet again. Janet and Bill stared out at the view for more than a minute, expecting further collapses, but it appeared that it was over again, for now. Bill leaned forward. She thought he was going to kiss her, but instead he used the sleeve of his shirt to wipe fresh blood away from her top lip.

*I hadn't even noticed I was bleeding.*

"That was too close," Janet said.

The sheriff looked along the road to the left, then back at Janet.

"That's something we can agree on. I was of a mind to sit it out and wait for the CDC to find us. But now I'm thinking we can't afford the time. I say we head back to the Western Road and take our chances again at the barricade."

Janet watched the smoke plume dissipate. If the collapse had been a hundred yards closer, there was more than a good chance that the bar, and all of the people in it, would already be gone.

"I think you're right," she replied. "I'd feel better to be on the move; at least it would feel like we were doing something, rather than just waiting to be swallowed up. And at least in daylight we've got more chance of avoiding the collapses."

Bill nodded, and ran a hand across her cheek.

"Chin up," he said. "It's time to tell the troops the

bad news."

They went back inside the bar. Janet called Fred and the girl through from the kitchen. Both of them looked pale and tired, but they said nothing as they joined the others, many of whom were now struggling up out of sleep.

When everyone was awake, the sheriff called for quiet.

"We plan on heading out," he said. "We need to get you folks to safety, and we're hoping the CDC will be more amenable now that they've had a chance to monitor the situation and get the lay of the land. I'm guessing somebody apart from the infantry we met last night will be in charge by now and they might at least listen to reason. But I ain't no dictator, and I don't want to lead you where you don't want to go, so I'll do what you all want."

Janet spoke up.

"I'm with the sheriff. Some of you need treatment I can't give you here. And there's a new hole formed just down the road. It's not safe to stay."

That statement brought a chorus of raised voices, but Janet was relieved to hear little dissent with the view that they should leave the bar.

"A show of hands then," the sheriff said. "Who wants to try our luck at the Western Road?"

There were only two dissenters, neither of whom was willing to stay behind on their own. Janet started to get them all moving when the sheriff called for silence again.

"Listen. I hear something."

Janet heard it too, a distant rumble that vibrated through the floor to be felt underfoot.

"It's back," someone shouted. "It heard us plotting."

They almost had a panic on their hands.

"Shut up and listen," Bill shouted, but they weren't in the mood to pay him any heed.

"We're going to get all ate up," someone shouted. People screamed, while others made a dash for the door. The sheriff took out his pistol and fired a shot into the ceiling. That got their attention quickly enough. The whole bar went quiet.

"I said, listen," Bill shouted.

The rumble resolved itself into the sound of heavy engines, getting closer fast.

"It's Ellen," somebody shouted. "The old bitch actually did it. We're saved."

The sheriff went back to the main door and looked out. Janet peered over his shoulder. A small convoy of military vehicles drove into the parking lot. Several of the trucks were mounted with heavy artillery.

*If this is getting saved, I'm not sure I want any part of it.*

It was a moot point anyway. There was no need to go looking for the CDC. The CDC had come to them.

* * *

The lead vehicle came to a halt and two men in HAZMAT suits got out, carrying a woman slumped between them. Fresh blood showed through a bandage round the person's head, and she didn't have to look up for Janet to recognize Ellen Simmons.

Janet tried to push past the sheriff, intent on going to the woman's aid, but Bill stood in her way and refused to budge. He pointed at the two men.

"They're carrying rifles across their backs. I ain't about to let you get yourself shot."

"Ellen needs help and…"

"And she'll be here in ten seconds. She can wait that long, until we see the lay of the land," he said. "Leave the talking to me."

The two suited men brought the injured woman right up to the door of the bar before they stopped.

"She'll be staying with you until we get the field camp set up," the one on the left said. "And I'll be taking your weapon, Sheriff."

"Like hell you will," Bill said. He reached for the pistol. Before he could finish the movement the two men in front of him had dropped Ellen Simmons to the ground and had weapons of their own in their hands. They had unslung and aimed the rifles so quickly that Janet had scarcely had time to register it.

"Don't do anything stupid, Sheriff," the one who had spoken previously said. "I'm not in the habit of killing civilians, and I've had about enough of it for one day."

Janet put a hand on Bill's arm.

"Do what they say. They've got a protocol, Bill. They're just following orders."

"That's what the Nazis said," the sheriff replied. He made a show of slowly taking his gun from the holster using only his fingertips, and dropped it at his feet.

Ellen Simmons tried to rise, stumbled, and fell. Bill crouched and caught her just before her head hit the ground. He helped her to her feet. She leaned against him. Her eyes rolled up to show only white, and she let out a pitiful moan.

"What did you do to her?" Bill said, anger clear in his voice.

"She'll live," the man in the HAZMAT suit said. He didn't seem to care either way. "And that's more than can be said for the three she had with her. She tried to drive through the barricade. She's lucky I don't just shoot her here and now and be done with it."

"And who are you?" Bill asked.

"General Frinton," the man said. "I'm the man in charge."

Janet doubted that very much, but held her tongue.

The other man bent and retrieved Bill's pistol, stowing it away in a deep pocket in his suit. Bill kept his attention focused on the general. The two men stared at each other for long seconds, and Janet felt tension build. Bill clenched and unclenched his fists. She saw the *need* to fight grow in him. She put a hand on his arm, he turned to look at her, and suddenly the tension dissipated as he managed a smile. He turned back to the general.

"So what happens now?" Bill asked.

"You sit tight. We're setting up a field camp and we'll get round to everybody in due course."

"But the holes..."

"We can have choppers here in seconds if need be."

*That might not be quick enough.*

"And what about the *apparitions*, the protoplasm?"

"We'll talk about that later," the man replied. Janet heard the skepticism in his voice. "For now, we've got a…"

"…protocol," Bill answered sarcastically. "I know."

"Stay inside until we call for you," the general said, turning away. "My men have orders to shoot anyone who tries to leave. I think you know by now that they'll have no qualms about doing so?"

Bill didn't reply at first, and when he spoke, it was slowly and deliberately.

"You're not going to kill any more of my people. I won't let you."

The general looked at first like he might reply angrily, then got control of himself.

"Just behave yourselves for a few hours more. This will all be over soon," he said.

The two men backed away towards their vehicles.

"Did things just get better, or worse?" Janet asked.

Bill didn't reply. He led them back into the bar and closed the door.

* * *

Ellen Simmons stood slumped against the wall, hands up to fend off the people crowded around her, all throwing questions, none waiting for an answer. Her face was white, her eyes red and wet. She'd been crying, and looked ready to start in again at any moment.

"Give us space," Janet shouted. "She needs my help."

Still nobody moved, not until Bill waded in and started shouting. Seconds later the space was clear. She led the woman to a corner table in the bar and

Bill kept the rest away. The head wound was the first priority. Janet carefully unwound the sodden bandages. The scalp wound underneath looked nasty, but it had already coagulated, and after she cleaned it up, looked to have little chance of further bleeding if Ellen could be kept still for long enough.

"What happened, Ellen?" she asked.

The other woman didn't answer. Her hands shook, and her lip trembled. She tried to speak, but nothing came out except a strangled moan.

"Charlie," Janet shouted. "We could do with some hard liquor over here."

Charlie took her at her word and arrived a minute later with two large measures of whiskey.

"It's a mite early in the morning," he said. "But my mother always said, a little of what you fancy does you the power of good."

Ellen Simmons looked up and almost managed a smile.

"I knew your mother," she said. "She whipped my ass for sassing her when I was no more than a slip of a girl. We could do with more like her with us here today."

She took the whiskey and knocked it back in one smooth gulp. Then she burst into tears.

"I'm sorry, Janet. I really am. I got those others killed. It was all my fault."

That was the only coherent sentence she uttered in the next five minutes. She drank most of Janet's whiskey too, and then lapsed into heaving sobs as Janet applied a fresh bandage to the head wound. She didn't look up when Janet patted her on the shoulder and left her to her grief. Several people started to move towards the older woman, as if intent on asking further questions.

"Leave her be," Janet said, possibly more sharply than she'd intended to. "She needs to rest."

To her surprise every one of them went back to their tables, leaving Ellen Simmons sobbing in the corner. After pausing to make sure they stayed where they'd retreated to, Janet joined the sheriff by the window. He didn't take his gaze off the activity outside.

"What are they doing?" she asked.

He didn't turn.

"What they said they would. Setting up a field camp. They've got all kinds of scientific kit, and the big trailer looks like a field lab to me. Ain't seen a single one without a HAZMAT suit on—or one without a weapon. Whatever they think is happening, they think it's *still* happening."

*I'm pretty sure I agree with them on that one.*

Once again she saw the anger in the sheriff, the need for action.

*It's eating him up, being locked in here.*

"They know what they're doing, Bill," she said softly.

"Killing my town, that's what they're doing," Bill replied. She moved to stand by his side, and finally saw why he hadn't turned. Tears streamed down his cheeks.

She reached up to brush them away but he gently stopped her.

"Don't," he said, quietly so only she would hear. "Don't let them know,"

She nodded, and put her hand down.

"I feel useless," Bill said. "Stuck in here while the

town goes to hell outside. What kind of sheriff does that make me?"

She moved closer to him, nose to nose, and spoke in a whisper, making sure he would read the anger in her eyes.

"Don't you dare," Janet said. "Self-pity doesn't fit you. You kept all these people alive last night. And we're all looking to you for more of the same. If you *dare* to turn pussy on us now, I'll kick your ass from here to California."

That got her a smile.

*It's a start.*

"So, man up, and get with the program, big guy," she said. "These folks here are scared. And you're the sheriff. It's your job to get them out of this. What's the plan?"

As she'd known it would, her barbs were enough to sting him into action. The sheriff looked her in the eye, kissed her full on the mouth, and turned to face the room.

"You all know who's out there," he said, loud enough for all to hear. "And you all know we ain't got much time for feds in this neck of the woods. But Doc here says that they know what they're doing, so we'll let them do their job. But I want you all to be ready to move fast if we need to. If another collapse starts, I want to be able to get out of its way. Are you with me on that?"

Everyone seemed to agree, and the arrival of the CDC had calmed some of those who seemed a little anxious. But there were many that only managed blank stares, and some had even gone back to sleep.

Janet was reminded of film of disaster victims;

blank stares, bandages, and a siege mentality.

*And that's just what we are now. Victims. Maybe later we'll be survivors. But I've got a feeling there's a way to go yet before then.*

* * *

"So what now?" Charlie asked. He poured himself another beer as he spoke, but Big Bill took it off him before he could start in on it and downed almost half of it in a single gulp.

"Now, you and I get some breakfast sorted out for these folks. It might be a long day, and a while before we get a square meal inside us. There'll be plenty of time for drinking later."

"Is that a promise?" Charlie said with a smile, but he gave the sheriff another salute, and followed as Janet and Bill went back through to the kitchen and checked out the contents of the store cupboards.

It was obvious they were not equipped for a long stay. The coffee at hand was enough for a couple of days, but by the time everyone had a breakfast the bread, milk and eggs would be mostly gone. The sheriff looked worried.

"I hope these CDC folks have a plan for feeding us, or moving us out, or both."

They rustled up a rudimentary breakfast of eggs and the last of a chunk of baloney, with as much coffee and toast as they could muster, and fed everyone that felt like eating. To Janet's dismay some of the folks didn't leave their seats, just sat, staring listlessly into space.

*They're close to giving up. It's just too much for them*

*to handle.*

After eating, some of the more mobile of the patients started to get agitated again.

"Come on, Bill. Do something," one of them said.

And Ellen Simmons, despite her ordeal of the night before, seemed to be getting back her spunk.

"If you don't get something moving, I will," she said to the sheriff.

Bill didn't answer, but Charlie laughed at her, which didn't help matters any.

"Go right ahead, Ellen. You got three folks killed last night. Want to try for more this time?"

Janet was afraid that Ellen might indeed march out the door and start making demands of the CDC, but it was a scenario they didn't have to worry about just yet, for before the woman could decide one way or the other, the CDC announced they were ready to begin.

* * *

It started with a knock on the door, so polite that Janet almost laughed out loud.

"Invite them in," Charlie shouted. "We can make some lunch and have a nice chat."

Bill answered the door. Two men, both of them carrying automatic rifles, stood outside.

"We're ready for you in the main trailer," one said. "One at a time, please."

"And what if we're not ready for *you?*" Bill asked. He got no reply, but both men tightened their grips on their weapons.

"We're ready for you," the other man said, his intent clear.

"And I don't suppose you're about to tell us what you're ready *for?*" Bill asked.

"Just some simple tests. No one will come to any harm."

Bill laughed in their faces.

"You ain't been paying much attention, have you, boy?"

Janet saw the man's grip tighten on his weapon.

*This could get ugly.*

She stepped forward to Bill's side.

"I'll go first," she said.

Bill shook his head.

"You're needed here," Bill replied. "The wounded are looking to you..."

"Which is why I have to go first," she said. "I need to show them there's nothing to worry about."

Bill wasn't happy with her decision, but she knew he'd see the sense of it. And she had another reason for going first. She hoped she would be able to reason with the CDC scientific and medical staff, and get them to investigate the more outlandish of the previous night's events.

As it turned out, she was only partially successful.

* * *

The two suited men escorted her the short distance across the parking area.

She saw three other suited figures inside the parked school bus, obviously taking samples and readings. She didn't get a chance for a closer look as they led her into the largest trailer of the three that had come up the road. One of her guards motioned that she should get inside. She stepped up into what proved to a laboratory a modest town doctor could only dream of having access to. Even a cursory examination of the gleaming surfaces and the kit that sat on them told her that many millions of dollars had been spent just in this one trailer.

Another suited figure was inside waiting for her.

"Come and sit down, Doctor," a soft female voice said. "This won't take long."

Janet couldn't see much of the woman's face through the visor, just blue eyes and a thin nose.

"And who might you be?"

"I'm Dr. Mullins. You've met the general, he's in charge of the security side of things. I've been landed with making sense of the science."

"I can help you there," Janet started. "You need to check down in the mines and..."

Mullins put up a hand.

"We can't act on anything you might tell us," she said. "Your perceptions can't be trusted in this kind of situation. As a doctor you know that?"

"But this is important..."

"And I'm sure you believe it. But last night we heard stories of Bigfoot, aliens, witches, ghosts, zombies, chupacabra and gremlins. All you'd be doing is adding another delusion to those we've already heard."

The import of what had just been said hit Janet just as she was about to complain.

"Last night? You talked to other townspeople?"

"Some," Mullins said. "We've managed to rescue a few people. They've all suffered some kind of breakdown, leaving them all with severe delusions. I suspect some kind of hallucinogen to be involved, given just how outlandish the stories seem."

"Those *stories* have a hint of truth to them if you'd only..."

The doctor sighed.

"Please. Just let me do my job?"

Janet started to reply, then thought better of it, seeing the futility of even trying. She let the scientist get on with it. Over the next twenty minutes she gave blood, stool, skin, urine, and hair samples. Small patches of material were snipped off her clothes, soil was scraped from the soles of her shoes, and no notice whatsoever was taken of anything she had to say.

"Just promise me that you'll keep an open mind," she said to Mullins once all of the prodding, poking and jabbing was done.

"That's also my job," the scientist said. "Trust me, we'll get to the bottom of this quickly. In the meantime, we'll assess your wounded as they come in. We'll quarantine any we think need more treatment than you can give them. Tell them not to worry. All of our equipment is state-of-the-art, and all of us have been trained specifically for situations like this."

*I doubt there have ever been any other situations like this one.*

"And the collapses?" Janet asked. "How do they fit into these *situations* you've been trained for?"

Even through the protective visor, Janet saw the first flicker of worry in the scientist's eyes.

"We have geologists looking into it," she said. "They're probably down there in one of the holes right now."

*Down there, and if I'm right, in mortal peril. But I'll never get this woman to believe it. Not until she sees it for herself.*

Janet decided to try a different tack.

"Would it be possible to see the quarantine area? If I see you're looking after folks properly, it'll make it easier for me to sell the idea on to those in the bar."

Mullins nodded.

"I can see the sense in that," she said. She turned her head inside her helmet and activated a comms device with her tongue.

*They've got communications. So at least something is still working, somewhere.*

She spoke too softly for Janet to hear, but the answer wasn't long in coming.

"The general has given me the go-ahead," the scientist said. "I'll take you over there now. We'll have to be quick...he gave me five minutes. But that should be more than enough time to put your mind at ease."

It did anything but put her at ease. Mullins led them to a large field tent. The last time Janet had seen anything like it in size had been on a visit to a circus as a teenager. But there was little fun to be had here. Suited and hooded figures moved between rows of beds. There were over fifty *patients*, in varying degrees of mobility. Janet knew some of them to speak to, and recognized others by sight. But they all had one thing in common; the same blank stare that Janet knew all too well from the bar, the stare of victims.

She scanned the faces hopefully, but found none from the convoy that had been lost in the road collapse.

"Where are the rest?" she asked, scaring herself with the hitch in her voice and the tears that threatened to come. Seeing just how few had made it through the night finally made her realize the scale of what had unfolded. Her knees went weak and she staggered, having to use one of the camp beds to prevent her from falling.

Mullins was as her side immediately, and Janet heard both concern and fear in her voice.

*She thinks I've been infected.*

Janet managed to stand up, stiffened her back, and wiped the tears aside.

"*Where* are the rest?" she asked again, more insistent this time.

"This is all," Mullins confirmed. "Apart from those of you in the bar, and the ones the general had stopped at the barricade."

"*Stopped?* That's a good word for it. *Murdered* is a better one."

The scientist said nothing.

*She disagrees with the general, on at least that point. That might be useful to keep in mind for later.*

"Have you seen enough?" Mullins asked seconds later.

Janet nodded. The patients were being treated well enough. But she'd also seen the armed guards at all of the exits, and the tension in the men carrying the weapons.

*There might be more folks getting stopped before the day is out.*

# 15

Fred came awake with a start. He and the girl, Sarah, had slumped together, each of them keeping the other upright. She slept through his wakening.

*And I didn't dream, so that's a bonus.*

He looked down at the top of the girl's head, at her mop of blonde hair. Although asleep, she still held his arm in a tight grip, and as he moved to change position her grip tightened, then loosened slightly when it was obvious he wasn't trying to move away.

*I don't even know this girl.*

But in a way, he did. He'd saved her life. And, although she didn't know it, she'd probably saved his, or at least stopped him from going crazy, just by being there beside him. At least she had stopped him thinking about another blonde, and another mop of hair, the last sight as she fell away into the blackness.

Black thoughts tried to creep back in. He managed to move enough that he was able to get a smoke out of his pocket and light up without disturbing the girl any further, and the everyday act of getting the cigarette lit and going was enough to calm his mind, for a time at least.

The girl moaned and snuggled closer when he leaned forward to flick some ash off his smoke. He fought off a sudden urge to pet her hair again. Now that it was full morning, and the *authorities,* such as they were, were parked outside, Fred felt slightly better with his current lot in life. That was improved further when the sheriff put a fresh mug of coffee in his hand and sat beside him.

"Give us one of them smokes, lad," the big man said.

Fred checked to make sure the sheriff wasn't joking.

"You ain't no smoker, Big Bill."

"Not since I was your age," the sheriff replied. "But today's special. It won't count." The big man said the last with a grin, and Fred was surprised to find that he was grinning back. He passed the sheriff a smoke and lit him up. They sucked smoke in silence, before the big man leaned in and whispered.

"You saw something out back, didn't you?" he said.

Fred didn't speak, couldn't get words to form.

"I saw it in your face," Bill said. "You saw something, right enough."

And there it was, just behind his eyes if he wanted to look, the old miner shuffling forward.

*Fred is dead.*

"Was it another demon?" the sheriff whispered.

Fred thought about that for a bit before answering.

"You know what, Sheriff? I think that's exactly what it was."

* * *

Doc came back seconds later, and Fred was amused to see the sheriff grind out his cigarette on her blind side and wave the smoke itself away with the back of his hand before turning.

"Your turn, Bill," Doc said. "And best leave the cigarettes here. It's a no smoking lab over there."

Bill grinned ruefully and gave Doc a peck on the cheek before leaving to join the armed men outside the door.

"So, what's up, Doc?" Charlie said, and got a laugh from most of those present which defused the tension that had been growing.

"They seem to know what they're doing," Doc said. "And there's some other folks from town over there in the big tent. We weren't the only ones to get out."

That statement caused a flurry of questions, about friends and family, that Doc was hard-pressed to answer. Some folks expressed a desire to move to the quarantine area, even after hearing Doc's misgivings. As Fred expected, Ellen Simmons wasn't one of them.

"I will *not* be held prisoner in my own town," she said, and looked around for support. Charlie gave her a mock salute from behind the bar, but that was the only answer she got, and she sat back down, a look of thunder on her face.

The sheriff came back not long after that.

Charlie surprised Fred by volunteering to go next. "Maybe they'll give me something for this headache," he said, pointing at the vivid wound on his scalp. "The booze stopped having any effect a while back."

Fred was further surprised to find himself fretting while the older man was gone, a gnawing worry sitting in his stomach that was only allayed when Charlie sauntered back in fifteen minutes later.

"Next!" he shouted.

One of the more seriously wounded went next, having to be helped by the guards in a slow shuffle to the trailer. He didn't come back. The guards walked across the parking bay ten minutes later and rapped on the door.

"He decided to go to quarantine," one of them said. "Who's next?"

Ellen Simmons looked like she wanted to say something, but a look from Big Bill quickly stopped her, and one of the other wounded took the next turn.

The morning passed slowly. Fred felt no compunction to move, and Sarah showed no sign of waking up. He held her close, checking every so often that she was all right, and watched the people leave for their checkups. Some came back, some didn't. Fred guessed they'd either been chosen, or even volunteered, for quarantine.

Ellen Simmons had other ideas, and after half a dozen had failed to return, she couldn't keep herself quiet any longer.

"It's a death panel, I'm telling you. We'll never see any of them again; they'll be dead and buried before you can say *Jack Robinson*."

Charlie said it before Fred could.

"Ellen, if you don't stop your mouth from running off, someone's going to stop it for you."

The woman was about to reply, but she chose that moment to look Charlie in the eye. There was something there she hadn't expected, something Fred hadn't seen before in the older man. There was a steely resolve, a certainty.

*The soldier he used to be is even stronger this morning.*

Fred was suddenly glad to be on Charlie's side of the fence. The face he'd looked into wasn't a man he wanted to mess with. It seemed Ellen Simmons had the same thought. She went quiet again.

The day wore on.

Finally there was no one else left who needed to get checked up.

"I already gave," Ellen Simmons said dryly when Doc looked at her.

"Your turn," Doc said to Fred.

He shook Sarah awake. There was a moment of panic in her eyes; then she looked up at Fred and smiled. Something melted in Fred's chest, and he held her tight.

"The government men want to have a look at us," Fred said. She stiffened at that, but he lifted her face up and looked her in the eye. "I ain't going to let anyone harm you. That's a promise. And I'll be with you the whole time. That's another promise."

They stood and went to the door.

"One at a time," one of the guards said.

"It's both of us or neither," Fred said.

"One at a time," the guard said again.

"I heard you the first time," Fred said. "So, neither it is." He turned to lead Sarah back into the bar, half expecting to be shot. The guard surprised him.

"Come on then, both of you. Let's get this over with."

Sarah maintained her clinging hold on him as they headed out across the parking bay.

* * *

Sarah stopped suddenly at the entrance to the trailer.

"I ain't too sure I want to do this," she said quietly. Fred heard one of the guards step closer behind them.

"I'm not going to let anything happen to you," he repeated.

"You'll save me from the bears?"

He nodded, unsure how to reply, but it seemed to be all she needed. Hand in hand, they went up into the trailer.

The scientist, Mullins, Doc had said her name was, seemed amused at their pairing until Fred reminded her of how he'd met the girl.

"How are you feeling?" the woman asked Sarah.

"Your storm troopers shot her parents and damned near killed her too. How do you *think* she's feeling?"

Things got a mite frosty after that. Fred endured the indignities of the tests. He had made a quick trip alone to the bathroom to collect his personal samples, wondering what mood the girl might be in on his return. She had been relatively calm then, but got increasingly agitated, and when she was asked to go alone to the small bathroom to give urine and stool samples, she refused point-blank to leave Fred's side.

"Come with me," she said, and looked up at him from eyes he was growing to realize he couldn't refuse.

"I'm not sure that's proper," the scientist said as Fred took Sarah by the hand and led her along the trailer.

"I'm not sure I give a fuck," Sarah said, and Fred had a big smile on his face as the girl led him into the bathroom.

* * *

There was only just enough space for the two of them to fit inside.

"Face the wall," the girl said, even managing a small, sad smile. "I need you here, but I don't need you seeing me do this."

Fred did as he was told and stood with his nose to the door. He couldn't plug his ears though, and he heard the sounds that accompanied her *sampling* clear enough. If Sarah was embarrassed at all, she didn't show it.

"All done," she said after a time. Wherever Sarah had been in her head, it seemed she was coming out of it. If Fred was worried that she might no longer need to lean on him, it was quickly quelled when she took his hand again as they left the bathroom. Sarah handed the samples to the scientist.

"You folks killed my ma and pa," she said dully. "I'm only helping you because you need it to help the others. It don't mean I like you, and when we get out of this, I'm going to be telling everybody that'll listen what you did."

"It wasn't me..." the scientist started, until Fred put up a hand.

"Right. You're only following orders. Tell it to your general. We're done with listening to you."

He led Sarah back to the bar. Her hand fit in his as if it belonged there.

# 16

The power in The Roadside gave out in midafternoon. Charlie had been trying to get a signal on the television above the bar. He jiggled the internal antenna, and at the same moment the lights went out.

"What did you do, old man?" the sheriff said.

"Weren't me, boss," Charlie replied. "I think a collapse might finally have took down the power lines out West."

"Is there a generator in the building?"

"Tony used to have one in the shed out back. Been a few years since he needed it, back during the last big blow. It might not be in tip-top order. Want me to have a look?"

"I'll go," the sheriff replied. "I need some air."

"Me too," Janet said, and got another withering look from Ellen Simmons that didn't bother her in the slightest. "Let's have at it, Bill. It'll be dark again before we know it."

"We should talk to the general," Ellen Simmons said. "Maybe they'll have a spare generator?"

"So now you want to talk to them?" the sheriff said. "Tell us again how well that's gone for us so far?"

It was only when Janet got the sheriff alone in the kitchen that he admitted the Simmons woman might, for once, have a point.

"At the very least, they'd surely take us all into the quarantine area," he said. "And that's certainly got its own generator."

"It's also got armed guards at every entrance," Janet reminded him. "I'd rather be somewhere with more chance of escape if things get hinky."

"*More* hinky, you mean?" Bill replied. "I agree, for myself, but I was thinking about the others. They might be better off with the CDC. And it's not just the electricity. We'll be needing to get folks fed soon, and the pantry is near empty."

Janet shook her head.

"They're following their *protocol*. It doesn't leave much room for individual judgement and snap decision-making. I agree we need to ask about the food, but I'm not keen on anything more than that. I'll take my chances in here with you, big man."

That got her a smile.

"Let's get to it then."

Bill paused as they reached the back door. Janet realized he was remembering how Fred had looked the last time the door was opened.

"It's daylight, Bill," she said softly. "We're safe."

As Bill turned the handle, opened the door and stepped outside, she hoped fervently that she was right. She followed him out into the yard.

* * *

Everything was quiet and peaceful. Janet found it almost impossible to stand there and believe the carnage that had taken place in the town. The trees in the rough country at the rear of the bar swayed gently in a cool breeze under a blue sky spotted with cotton wool clouds. High above a passenger jet laid a white line across the blue.

*They have no idea what's going on down here.*

The storage shed sat on the other side of the yard, past the rusting pickup truck. As they walked around the discarded vehicle, something seemed to shift and move in the shadows in the passenger seat, but when Janet looked again, she saw nothing there but darkness. She noticed Bill tense up slightly, and his hand reached for where his pistol would have been before he stopped himself.

"Stay close," he said softly.

It got noticeably colder as they approached the shed. The old, battered door opened at the second attempt, swinging inward with a creak to reveal a dark, windowless room beyond. Bill went first.

"Be careful," Janet said. She whispered, afraid to speak too loudly, and her flight-or-fight mechanism kicked in. Her heart rate went up, and every sense seemed heightened. Bill stepped inside the shed. She followed close behind.

It took her eyes several seconds to adjust. Something skittered along the far wall, and she nearly leapt into Bill's arms in fright before she saw the mouse, its pink tail giving a final flourish as it went down a hole in the flooring. Apart from that, nothing else moved in the shed other than dust motes glinting where the sun shone in through the door.

The space served as storage for anything the bar wasn't currently using, or had used up. Broken chairs, wobbly tables and bashed cabinets piled higgledy-piggledy against the far wall. They found a generator, and six twenty-liter containers of gasoline under a broken tabletop to the side of the door. A thick layer of dust covered everything.

"Give me a hand here," Bill said, taking one of the canisters. "We can hook this up at the back of the kitchen. There's enough gas here to last us a while."

They ferried the six canisters back to the kitchen door, and returned for the generator. They had managed to get it as far as the open doorway when Janet felt a vibration—first in the soles of her feet, then at her jaw. Bill's nose dripped two large spots of fresh blood down onto his shirt. The darkness in the corner of the shed thickened and seemed to coalesce. Bill grabbed her by the arm and dragged both her and the generator out into the sunlight, but not before she'd seen the old man in the corner; a miner by the looks of things.

"Fred is dead," a thick voice said dully from the shadows.

Then she was back in the sunshine in the yard, watching the dust on the ground dance, waiting for a collapse to swallow them up.

It never came.

The ground trembled, clumps of earth dancing like dust on a loudspeaker. Then, as quickly as it had come, the hum faded and died. The trembling ground stilled.

"Are we still here?" Bill said, wiping more blood from his upper lip onto the sleeve of his shirt.

Janet didn't take her eyes off the shed doorway. The shadows inside seemed to shift and sway, but there was no sign of any old miner, and no more voices. Eventually she forced herself to look away and turned to face Bill.

"Let's get this generator hooked up," Janet said. "If we're staying the night in the bar, I want it to be well lit."

* * *

Charlie and Bill got the generator working after a bit of elbow grease and a long bout of cursing. Janet stood to one side, watching the shadows move in the yard outside the open back door.

*The light's fading fast.*

"Give it a try now," Bill shouted, surprising her into an involuntary twitch. She reached over and flicked the switch nearest her. The lights in the kitchen flickered on and off, then came full on and steadied. The generator throbbed noisily and annoyingly here at the rear of the kitchen, but it was a small price to pay for the comfort of the lights.

"And we've got enough propane to burn the stoves and rings for a while," Charlie said. "Ain't much to cook though. I found some tins of beans and there's three loaves defrosting from the chest freezer.

That's about it, although there's plenty of packs of peanuts and chips behind the bar."

"I don't think we have to worry about junk food killing us, do you?" Janet said, and Charlie laughed so loud and hard that Janet found herself joining in. Bill rose from the generator and raised an eyebrow.

"What's so funny?"

For some reason that amused both Janet and Charlie, so much they couldn't answer for laughing. There might have been more than a hint of hysteria in it, but Janet felt much better as she moved to close the back door. She had one last look outside, but there was nothing to see but the empty yard, and she didn't look too closely at the shifting shadows in the pickup truck or at the still-open shed door.

* * *

The three of them went back though to the main bar.

Fred and the girl still sat shoulder to shoulder at a table, and Ellen Simmons sat on her own in the corner. There was no one else in the bar. The dozen people who had been there before Janet and Bill went to get the generator were gone, taking any good humor Janet might have felt with them.

"What the hell happened?" she asked.

"They got spooked at that last hum," Fred said. "They decided to take their chances with the CDC. They had a vote and everything."

Janet went to the front door. It lay open. She looked out to see the CDC guards enter the quarantine tent. The canvas flaps slid back into place, and it was as if they'd never been there at all. There was no sign of any of the people from the bar.

Janet felt bereft, as if some of her reasons for being there at all had just been taken from her. Worse, she felt as if she'd been personally betrayed. Tears ran down her cheeks, a mixture of anger, rage and self-pity.

*They were my patients, damn it.*

She turned back to Bill.

"So what now? Still staying?"

The sheriff didn't speak, just led her back inside the bar and closed the door behind them. She put an arm around his waist. Ellen Simmons smirked again.

"You got anything to say, Ellen?" the sheriff asked.

The older woman smiled thinly.

"Only that I can see you all coming round to my way of thinking. Ain't no use us getting cozy with the CDC; that way will only get us dead. We should sneak out of town under cover of darkness tonight."

Charlie laughed.

"*Under cover of darkness?* You've been watching too much television, Ellen. And ain't you been paying attention here? Seems to me that it's the darkness that's trying to kill us."

"Don't talk such garbage, old man," Ellen Simmons said. "The liquor has addled you."

A small voice spoke up.

"No. He's right. They only come in the dark." Sarah Bennett looked up from where she'd rested her head on Fred's shoulder. "The bears like the dark."

Ellen Simmons laughed, and Janet saw the flash of anger that crossed Fred Grant's face.

*I need to defuse this, and fast.*

The sheriff beat her to it.

"The kid's right, Ellen. We've all seen them now. Whether they're devils, haunts or something man-made from the mines, I know now they're real—as real as you or me. And they come in the dark."

Ellen Simmons still looked skeptical. Janet came to a quick decision.

"Charlie. Fetch us some drinks. We're going to have this out once and for all."

* * *

Five minutes later they all sat around one of the bar's bigger tables, with drinks and a selection of nuts and chips on the table. It felt absurdly like just any other get-together. But the subject matter of conversation was not so matter-of-fact.

"I'm telling you, it was a miner," Fred said. "And I think it was one of old Charlie's dead work mates."

Charlie went white at that, but didn't speak, just gulped down a stiff shot of JD and went to the bar for another.

"I believe you," Janet replied. "I saw him too."

She went on to tell of their encounter earlier in the shed. Then Bill told of his *demons*, and spoke of the strange apparition of a flying saucer. Sarah muttered something else about bears but refused to go into detail.

"Charlie. Do you want to talk about what you saw in the kitchen?"

"Nope," the man said. "But if it weren't VC, then I don't know what they were."

"Hinky," Bill said, and dropped Janet a wink.

"That's what they were. Show-and-tell time, Ellen. And we've shown ours."

"You're all mad," the older woman said. "I'm having nothing to do with this."

She started to stand, but stopped when Janet spoke.

"So, you're telling us you didn't see a biker gang?"

The older woman sat back down, hard.

"That was different," she said, then went quiet.

"No, I don't think it was," Janet replied. "I'm not sure what we're up against here, but I'm pretty sure its cause is down in the depths of these collapses somewhere. It's no coincidence it started the same time as the problems at Hopman's Hollow. I'm also not sure that they mean us any harm."

Charlie looked up at that. She remembered him, on his knees on the kitchen floor.

*But had he put himself there? Was it only his own fear that had crippled him?*

"So what do we do about it?" Fred asked.

*That's the $64,000 question.*

"I want to try an experiment," she said. "Once it gets dark. I think all of these manifestations are something trying to communicate with us. Maybe it's time we started listening. Maybe even talking back."

She saw on the others' faces that they weren't convinced. But none of them, not even Ellen Simmons, argued with her.

*We all know it's the only way forward.*

* * *

They had no other contact with the CDC all afternoon, and Janet was starting to think they would be left alone for the night when two suited figures came to the front door of the bar.

"We're here for the lady, Doc," one said.

"Well that ain't gonna happen," Bill replied. Janet nudged him aside.

"It's okay, Bill. Let's just see what they want."

"Dr. Mullins wants to see you," the guard said.

"What about?"

That didn't get an answer.

*Protocols.*

Bill was all for closing the door in their faces.

"They don't get to order us around. Not in my town."

Janet put a hand on his arm.

"It's Mullins that has asked for me, not the general. It could be something medical they need me for; a problem with one of the wounded. Stay here, have a beer. I'll be back before dark, that's a promise." She leaned over and kissed him full on the lips. "And that's another one."

She had her back to the table as she left the bar, but could well imagine the expression on Ellen Simmons' face, and she wore a grin as they went across the parking lot to the trailer that housed the laboratory.

The grin lasted only as long as it took for Mullins to show her what they had on a gurney.

# 17

Fred was left alone with the girl. Ellen Simmons had taken herself back to her place in the far corner, while Bill and Charlie were in a huddled conversation over a couple of bottles of beer at the bar itself. Sarah sat as close to him as she could get despite all the empty space around them.

Fred lit up a smoke and sipped from a JD that Charlie had left on the table.

"We could join the others," he said. "In quarantine. Let the CDC look after us?"

She lifted her head and looked into his eyes.

"That's your job now," she said, and kissed him on the cheek. "And in case you hadn't noticed, you've made a pretty good start."

He smiled back at her, and it felt so good he left the expression there for a while.

"Yes, ma'am," he replied. "Service with a smile."

She put her head against his shoulder and started to sob quietly.

"I miss them," she said. "They ain't ever coming back. And it were those bastards in the suits what did it. I'll never trust them. For all I know it were them that sent the bears to the farm."

She'd mentioned the bears several times now. Fred guessed they were her *thing*, like his with ghosts, and Doc's with aliens.

"Tell me about the bears," he said softly. That was all it took. Sarah started speaking, and it all came out in a rush.

"It were just after dark," she started. She took his cigarette from him, her hand trembling, and smoked in tiny puffs, not inhaling, an amateur pretending to be a smoker. It did seem to calm her though, so Fred let her keep it and lit up another for himself. "Pa was out in the barn and Ma was in the kitchen. I was in the parlor, just sitting and thinking.

"And that's when I done heard it, a *snuffling* and a *scratching*, like a 'coon trying to find a way in. Pa came back from the barn and went straight to the gun cabinet. He had his shotgun out and loaded seconds later. 'Stay here,' he said. 'Damn 'coons are at it again.'

"He went outside and we heard him stomping and cursing for a long time. But there weren't anything for him to shoot at…not right then.

"We sat in the kitchen for an hour. The things snuffled and scratched, but every time Pa went looking, there weren't nothing there for him to shoot at. Ma was getting herself into a right state. She thought it was rats. And if there's one thing Ma can't stand, it's rats. 'Kill them, Pa,' she screamed. 'Kill them all.'

"Pa was right riled up after a while of Ma's shouting, and he was good and ready to shoot first and ask questions later.

"So when the handle started to turn on the back door, he let off the shotgun. Blew the window right out and everything.

"'Got you now, fuckers,' he shouted and ran to the door. Ma and me were right behind him, hoping to see that he'd got the booger that had us so afeart.

"But there weren't nothing there. Ma got sorely spooked at that, and started screaming for Pa to get us out of there. Pa weren't for leaving though. He loaded up that big old gun again and went running round the farm. Me and Ma heard him blasting away at anything that moved. I done told Ma that everything was okay, that Pa would protect us.

"But when Pa came back, he was as white as a sheet.

"'Phone your sister and tell her we're heading her way. Then get your coat on,' he said to Ma. 'We have to go. Right now.'

"'What's wrong, Pa?' I asked. I thought he weren't gonna answer, and when he did, he didn't sound like Pa at all. He sounded like a scared old man.

"'Summat's taken the barn. Ate it all up. There ain't nothing left but a big hole in the field.'

"Of course, I didn't believe him—not right then. I tried to push him aside, but he wouldn't let me see.

"'Just for once, do as you're told, lass,' he said. He was so quiet, so gentle, I knew summat was wrong. 'We need to get out of here.'

"At least Ma did as she was told. She was good at

that. She put the phone down.

"'She's expecting us in a couple of hours. I need to pack…'

"'Ain't no time for no packing,' Pa said. 'We're leaving now.'

"Pa made us walk behind him out onto the front porch. He fired again, near deafened me, at a shadow near the truck. When I looked, there weren't nothing there but fresh spattering of pellets in the bodywork.

"'What is it, Pa?' Ma asked.

"'Haunts.' That was all he'd say. He bundled us into the truck, and we bounced away over the ploughed field. I thought my teeth was going to rattle right out of my head."

The girl leaned forward to stub out the cigarette she'd been holding without smoking. Her hand trembled so much she could scarcely reach the ashtray. Fred took the smoke gently from her fingers and ground it out.

"You don't have to go on," he said. "Not if you don't want to."

She looked up at him, fresh tears in her eyes.

"I need to tell you," she said. "The bears might come back."

She wiped the moisture from her eyes angrily, then continued her story.

"Ma saw the bears first; four of them, blocking the gate to the field.

"'Pa!' she screamed.

"'I see them,' Pa replied. He floored the pedal of the old truck and headed straight for them…and you ain't gonna believe this bit.

"The headlights washed over the bears and they

started to *melt.* Then we hit them, straight on. Suddenly the whole windshield was covered in red *gloop*, like summat from one of them horror films. Ma screamed fit to burst, and Pa cussed and swore like a sailor. Then, finally, the wipers done did their job and our view cleared. When we got to the highway, Pa still had his foot down, hard. Something started to rattle at the back axle and he had to slow, but not too much.

"Ma clung so tight to me I couldn't hardly breathe, and Pa kept cussing, long after we'd left the farm behind.

"'I think we're clear,' he said, finally. 'Ain't nothing on this road but us.'

"'What was it, Pa?' Ma said. 'What did we hit?'

"He didn't answer, just lit up a smoke, but I saw by the way his hands shook that he weren't near as calm as he pretended to be.

"At first Pa meant to head for town, but as we crested Parson's Hill we saw all the lights go out across the trailer park. Pa braked hard at the same time, damned near sent me through the windshield. I weren't allowed the time to chew him out though. Three more bears came out of the woods. Ain't like no bears I seen afore; these were big and red and soft. But they were bears all right. What else could they be?

"And they done died easily enough. Pa leaned out his window and shot one in the head and it just burst and fell apart like a water balloon. Then we were headed off back along the road, making for the forest track and we got stopped by the men in the white suits..."

She stopped again, and grabbed Fred's free hand.

"You can guess the rest. Pa weren't in no mood to obey no feds…not after the thing with the bears.

"'Ain't going back to no town,' he said. 'Not if there ain't any town to go back to.'

"He gunned the engine, I heard a shot…and the next thing I remember is seeing your face as you leaned over me."

She had fresh tears running down her cheeks, but didn't stop Fred when he wiped them gently away.

"I'll take the job," he said. "I won't let anything happen to you."

She smiled wanly.

"Maybe you ain't got any choice in the matter."

# 18

The laboratory was in semidarkness, and at first glance Janet wasn't sure what she was looking at on the trestles. They looked like giant heads of corn, some six feet long, over a foot in diameter, but they were pink where corn would have been green; pink and wet, like flesh. As she got closer she saw they were translucent, and contained rounded, unformed embryos.

Then she got it.

*Pod people. Somebody's thing is pod people.*

Mullins pointed at the pods.

"Is this the same material you told me about?"

"Put on the lights and you'll see for yourself quickly enough."

"I don't have to do that. I've got some on a slide."

Mullins pointed Janet over to a microscope. She looked down, and saw exactly what she expected to see. The illuminated mount gave out enough light for the *sample* to revert to the basic protoplasm she'd seen in her own surgery.

Mullins was bent over a trestle, examining the pods.

"The geologists we sent down to check out the mines found them. They say the whole system is full of them; hundreds, they said."

Janet tried to gauge the scientist's emotional state, but couldn't read anything through the facemask.

"I told you when I was here before. These are just a manifestation," Janet said. "One of the geologists has a *thing* for Pod People, that's all. You could just as easily have found the nest of a giant spider. Indeed, you might well do just that the next time you go down there."

"Nobody's going down there," Mullins said. "The general is going to burn the place out, just as soon as it can be arranged."

"I suspect that won't cure anything," Janet said. "You people are now as much infected as we are. You just haven't noticed it yet."

"Nonsense. We've taken every precaution."

"And it's not enough. But you'll be finding that out for yourself when it gets dark."

Mullins went quiet at that. Now that she had the scientist thinking, Janet pressed her advantage.

"And if you don't want a mutiny on your hands, I suggest you get some supplies over to us. There's only six of us now, but we're running out of food."

Mullins nodded, although she had a faraway look in her eyes. Janet didn't want to push too hard. She stood, and Mullins let her walk away.

"Now excuse me," she said as she went down out

of the trailer. "I have an experiment of my own to prepare."

# 19

"Are you sure this is wise?" Bill said.

It had grown dark outside. The CDC had the parking lot lit up with arc lights, but here at the back of the bar the gloom thickened and shadows crept. Janet stood at the open kitchen door, looking out into the backyard.

"The CDC is no better off than we are," Janet said. "And the general's answer is to bomb the shit out of it. I'm sure *that's* not wise."

She turned to look at the sheriff. They were the only two at the door, the others having turned down a chance to watch Janet's *experiment* in favor of staying in the bar. They'd left Fred and the girl in conversation, Ellen Simmons in her corner, and Charlie behind the bar with a fresh bottle of JD. Here at the kitchen door the only sound came from the constant beat of the generator.

Janet leaned against Bill. He put an arm around her and pulled her close. They stood like that for a long time, neither speaking, as the darkness gathered in the yard outside.

Shadows shifted in the passenger seat of the rusting pickup. Night fell. Somebody sat in the pickup, staring back at Janet and the sheriff, unmoving, as yet.

"It's showtime," Bill whispered.

"Shush. I'm concentrating."

The figure swung itself out of the seat. The legs flowed and thickened, becoming pale, naked and strangely thin, with three toes on each shoeless foot. The too-thin body rolled out of the pickup, languidly, smoothly, with all the grace of a practiced dancer. It stood in front of them, unblinking, five-foot-high arms too long in proportion to its height. The slender oval head tilted to one side. Large oval eyes—all pupil and blacker than the surrounding shadow—stared straight at Janet. The thing raised a hand that contained two long fingers and a thumb and spoke from a mouth that was little more than a slit across the lower part of its face.

"Fred is dead," it said.

Janet took a deep breath and stepped out of Bill's arms to stand directly in front of it. She had no real plan of action in mind beyond attempting communication. She held up her right hand to mimic the thing's gesture, and spoke.

"Fred is dead," she said.

"We are with Fred," it replied. Janet watched carefully, but there were no accompanying hand or head movements that might give away what it meant or what it wanted in reply.

"We are with Fred," she answered, hoping that she was saying the right thing and not just making matters worse for them.

"Fred is dead."

*This is getting us nowhere.*

At the corner of her eye she saw something else shift in the dark inside the pickup. There was something else in the passenger seat.

"Janet," Bill whispered behind her.

"I see it," she said, softly.

The thing in front of her cocked its head at the sound.

*At least I know it reacts to me and it's not just some kind of recording.*

She stepped closer and opened her arms, showing her palms.

"We mean no harm."

"Weemean," it replied, and opened out its palms to her. At the same time a second pale figure stepped down out of the pickup. It too spoke.

"Weemean."

"Janet," Bill said behind her. "This isn't fucking *Close Encounters*. Get back here."

"Weemean," a third one said as it stepped out of the shed. Two more came into the yard from out of the trees. Once all five were together, they advanced on Janet.

She tried to force down her fear; the nights spent hiding under covers, too scared to look out in case the *Grays* had come for her. There were other times too, when she'd run home in the gloom, scared that a sudden bright light overhead might lead to her being sucked up and away into the sky. Silly girlish worries from a time long past...but all too real here in the dark of the yard.

"Janet!" Bill said, and she heard the fear and worry in that one word. She ignored him, and held her ground as the *Grays* gathered around her.

"We mean you no harm," she said softly.

"Weemean," the five said in unison.

The closest one reached out and stroked Janet's arm. Pain hit her, as if a red-hot poker had been drawn across her skin, the burn coming up immediately in a six-inch, pencil-thin line. She drew her arm away as another *Gray* reached for her.

"Weemean," the five said, and closed in. One of them grabbed her on the wrist, long fingers circling all the way round, bringing a new flare of pain that was almost unendurable. Janet screamed.

The five *Grays* backed off, as if confused.

"Weemean," they said.

Janet could barely speak through the pain.

"What do you want?"

She felt Bill's hand on her shoulder.

"What do you want?" she shouted.

They cocked their heads to one side.

"Weemean."

They came forward again, long fingers reaching out, as if needing to touch her. When Bill dragged her away, she let him do it.

"Weemean," the *Grays* said, and came after them.

"Eat shit and die," a voice replied. Charlie stood in the doorway, waving the flashlight, passing the beam over the pale forms. Where the light hit they melted and flowed. Thin wisps of dark smoke rose from the liquefying flesh.

"Weemean," they whispered, and as one collapsed into a bubbling mess on the dirt. Within seconds there was nothing left of them, just wet ground and thin smoke that quickly dissipated in the breeze.

* * *

The ache in her arm from the two distinct burns didn't start to ease until she'd swallowed three strong painkillers from her kit and downed a decent slug of JD. Even then the burns throbbed and beat beneath the bandages and salve she had applied. The wrist was the worst. Her flesh, what remained of it, had blistered and split—the marks where each of the thing's fingers had gripped showed as bloody weals. She'd made sure Bill did not see the full extent of the damage as she bandaged it, but that didn't stop him fretting over her.

"We need to get you over to the quarantine room," Bill said. "They can take care of that..."

"I can take care of it myself," she said, rather too sharply, and immediately regretted the look of pain she had brought to the sheriff's face. "Look, Bill. If I go over there, I'd have to stay there. In case you haven't noticed, nobody comes out. At least here we have a chance of responding if anything happens, if the hum comes back..."

She stopped, struck by a sudden thought.

*I didn't notice that.*

Bill raised an eyebrow.

"I know that look. You've thought of something?"

She nodded.

"There was no hum. When they came this time, there was no hum. Maybe the two phenomenon aren't as closely linked as we thought?"

"Does that help us?"

"I don't see how just yet. But it might."

"Did you learn *anything?*"

She thought about that.

"Maybe," she said, holding up her bandaged arm. "I don't think they knew what they were doing. I didn't get any impression they meant me harm."

Bill shook his head.

"Apart from burning you to the bone, you mean?"

"As I said, I don't think they meant it. I think they were trying to make contact."

"Well, they did that well enough. What now?"

Janet realized something else. At some point, Bill had stopped being the titular *person in charge,* and the mantle had passed to her. Bill needed something to do, he just didn't have any reference points in his past to tell him what that might be.

*And neither do I.*

But the sheriff was looking at her, still waiting for an answer.

"We don't know how long we'll be here," she said. "Let's see if we can rustle up some hot food and coffee. It could be a long night."

That was enough to get Bill moving. She went after him, and together they made toast and enough coffee for two mugs for everybody should they want it. They set it out on the table they'd all sat at earlier. Fred and Sarah immediately started in on the toast, but Ellen Simmons, initially at least, seemed reluctant. She didn't leave her seat in the corner.

"How do I know it's not drugged? This could be a trick to make sure I go quietly to the CDC quarantine."

Charlie came out from behind the bar with a fresh beer in his hand.

"Ellen, if we wanted you unconscious, we'd just hit you on the head. Come on over here and join us. I'll even taste it first if you're that paranoid?"

Hunger got the better of her, and Ellen Simmons finally joined them, sitting next to Charlie, the two of them sharing both toast and Charlie's beer. They all ate sitting round the big table, and while it wasn't exactly convivial, it was as close to routine as they had managed since the disaster unfolded.

"What's the plan, Big Bill?" Charlie asked.

Bill immediately looked to Janet and raised an eyebrow.

*Looks like I'm up.*

"I thought that sitting tight might be our best hope," she began. "But now I'm not so sure." She held up her arm, showing the rest of them the fresh bandages. "These things we've been seeing are more than simple haunts. They can touch us, burn us. We *should* be okay as long as we stay in the light, but even that's an assumption on my part, and that's dangerous."

"So what do we do?" Fred asked.

"I say we make a run for it," Ellen Simmons said. Charlie laughed again.

"As I said before, Ellen, you've been watching too much cheap television. We're up against folks with automatic weapons for a start, and God knows what else will come up out of them holes. What do you suggest we use to fight back? A big stick?"

"We could sneak out the back..." Fred said.

The sheriff shook his head.

"It's not safe in the dark. I think we can all agree on that."

Everyone around the table went quiet until Ellen Simmons spoke up again.

"So that's it? We sit here and wait for whatever's coming to us?"

Nobody replied.

*We're out of ideas. And running out of time.*

* * *

Matters were taken out of their hands minutes later. Fred and Charlie had just lit up post-meal cigarettes when they all heard movement outside the front door. Bill waved a hand, asking for quiet, and moved quickly to the door, just as someone turned the handle. Bill pulled the door open.

A slim woman stood there.

*She's not wearing a suit.*

It took Janet a second before she recognized the scientist, Mullins. The newcomer walked into the bar and smiled thinly.

"The good news is that all your tests came back clean. The general has told me to get you ready to move out. The wounded are already on their way out of town. You're next."

Janet went to the door and looked out, just in time to see two long trucks drive out of the parking lot and away out of sight in the darkness.

"Is that wise?" Janet asked. "What about our

*shared* experiences and…"

Mullins interrupted her.

"There's no physical evidence of anything wrong with you," she said. "And the general wants to get on with clearing this mess up. You're moving out."

"Whether we like it or not?" Charlie said.

Mullins nodded.

"The general isn't a man to change his mind once it's made up. And believe me, you'll be safer as far away from here as you can get."

*Now that's something I can believe.*

To no one's surprise, Ellen Simmons was the first to move.

"It's about time too," she said. "Get me out of here. I've got a reporter to find."

Before they left, the sheriff went through the back and switched off the generator.

"We might yet be coming back," he said dryly when he returned. Janet herded everyone else out into the parking lot, grateful that it was well-lit by the CDC's arc lights. She saw that the quarantine area was the only spot that sat in darkness.

"Do we take the bus?" Charlie asked. Janet saw that the older man had a full bottle of JD in one hand, and the flashlight in the other.

"No," Mullins said. "We have something a bit more secure."

She led them round the trailer that housed the laboratory. A long, armored troop carrier sat in the corner of the lot, headlights on and engine running. Two men sat up front, a driver and a soldier who made a point of showing them that he had an automatic rifle in his arms.

"For protection," Mullins said without a hint of irony, and started to shepherd them inside the truck. There were three long seats with a narrow walkway up the left-hand side. Fred and the girl went in the front nearest the driver, Charlie and Ellen Simmons in the middle. Janet pushed Bill up to the rear and got in beside him. Mullins sat beside Fred, just behind the armed man.

"We'll have you out of here in no time," the scientist said. She pulled the truck door shut. "All present."

The driver put the truck in gear and they headed out into another night.

* * *

Bill surprised Janet by taking her hand.

"We shouldn't be going," she said softly. "We should be staying, examining whatever it was we *almost* communicated with."

Bill's grip on her hand tightened.

"Leave it to these guys," he said. "I just want you out of harm's way."

"These guys are just going to bomb the shit out of it," Janet said. "We might be looking at something completely new to our experience. And it will be lost forever."

Bill reached over and turned her face round to look her in the eyes.

"Janet. It took my town…our town. It has killed God knows how many people. And it damned near burned through your arm just an hour ago. And I *still* ain't convinced we're not dealing with demons straight from the gates of hell. Maybe it's best just to let the general do what he's gotta do?"

*Best for whom?*

She leaned her head on Bill's shoulder and closed her eyes, suddenly weary.

The truck had a better suspension than the old bus, the smoothness of the ride bringing some degree of security to the journey. But now they were out of the bar Janet felt exposed, her fears threatening to grip her. She saw them again in her mind's eye; the too-thin, too-pale figures, reaching for her with fingers that were almost skeletal.

"Fred is dead."

She heard the phrase in her mind, and at the same time, became aware of fresh wetness at her lip. Her jaw vibrated and a shiver ran the length of her spine.

*We're in trouble.*

# 20

Fred was grateful for one thing. He'd let Sarah get into the truck first. That at least meant that he was between her and the scientist, Mullins.

*If they'd sat together, they might be at blows by now.*

Even as it was, Sarah was starting to let her anger build up a head of steam.

"So what's she going to do now?" Sarah said, making sure Mullins wasn't going to be able to ignore her. "Take us out to a field and shoot us in the head? Or maybe just throw us down a hole? What *orders* does she have this time?"

Fred was starting to wish he'd followed Charlie's example and filched a bottle of JD from behind the bar. Getting between two women in a fight was never a good idea at the best of times.

*And now ain't anywhere close to the best of times.*

"My only job here is to make sure you get to safety," Mullins said.

"Like you did with Ma and Pa?" Sarah said, her voice rising so that she was close to a shout. "They're sure *safe* now, ain't they?"

Mullins kept looking straight ahead. Fred guessed that she couldn't look them in the eye.

"I've told you before, that wasn't me..."

"Yeah, you said. I ain't seen you coming over to our side yet though."

"It's not a question of sides. We're all in this together."

"Give me a gun then," Sarah said. "Let's see how far this *togetherness* goes."

The armed guard in the passenger seat up front turned and showed Sarah his rifle.

"If you don't keep quiet, you'll get a closer look at this gun than you'd like."

Sarah didn't flinch.

"I'll make it easy for you," she said and started to rise from her seat. "I'll just get off here."

The girl tried to push past Fred, just as the truck hit a bump, and she fell into his lap. Fred smiled, but Sarah looked like she might slap him.

"Let me go," she said...just as she was hit by a nosebleed that dripped in a constant stream down her shirt. Fred tasted blood at his lips, felt the vibration shake along his jaw.

*We're in trouble again.*

"Brace yourself," he said to Sarah. She grabbed him tight, her face buried against his chest. Fred looked past her. He had a clear view through the gap between their driver and the armed man up front, and soon wished he hadn't.

The road crumbled, falling in slow motion, down

into darkness. The driver tried to haul the truck aside, but was too slow. The front wheels went over the edge and the truck tipped forward. If Fred had been driving, he'd have thrown the vehicle into reverse, but he saw immediately that he'd only have managed to tip the truck over. Instead their driver went with the collapse, accelerating into it, driving down into the hole, skidding and sliding on a loose bed of dirt and gravel that accompanied their descent.

The headlights showed them getting deeper into a narrowing crevice, one that was also getting steeper, until the driver lost control of the truck completely and they were carried down, bucking and swaying, on a monstrous roller-coaster ride to hell.

* * *

Sarah clung so tightly that Fred felt his chest constricting, and he struggled for breath. The headlights suddenly picked out a wall of rock, looming ahead of them, filling the view. The driver slammed on the brakes. They didn't slow. The truck hit the wall headlong in a crash of tortured metal and glass, throwing the passengers around like so many rag dolls.

Fred's head hit something, hard. He tasted more blood in his mouth and could see only blackness. He was now breathing more freely, but that only meant Sarah no longer held on to him.

"Sarah!" he shouted, but heard no response. He felt dizzy, and when he pushed, tried to move, his muscles didn't reply.

*Fred is dead.*

A flash of light told him that wasn't quite true.

Something shifted in the darkness, and he felt a hand at his cheek.

"Sarah?"

"I'm here."

"Keep talking," someone else said. "I'll get to you."

The light moved and bobbed.

"Charlie?"

"That's me," the older man said. "Anybody else here?"

"We're in one piece back here," Janet replied from somewhere behind them. "Mullins?"

There was no reply to that one.

"Anybody up front?" Charlie asked. There was no reply to that either.

"I'm still here, if anybody cares," Ellen Simmons said.

"Can anybody get out?" Charlie said.

Something shifted at Fred's right, and Mullins spoke, her voice clearly showing she was in some pain.

"Shine that light over here," she said.

Charlie did as she asked. The beam hit her face, and Fred got a good look at her. Blood poured from her nose and ears and her eyes fluttered.

"Doc. We're going to need you," Fred said.

"Nobody move," Mullins replied, although the act of speaking was clearly causing her great pain. "I've got the door if I can get more light on it?"

Charlie moved the beam towards the truck door.

"That'll do it," Mullins said. She slid the door open, leaned over…and fell out of the truck into the darkness. There was a soft thud as she hit ground outside.

Fred felt Sarah move away from him, heading for the open doorway.

"Charlie, get over here. We've got a problem."

"Just the one?" the older man said. The flashlight beam shifted again, and a couple of seconds later Charlie climbed his way out of the door. Now that Sarah's weight was off him, Fred found he could shift himself easily enough.

He climbed out of the truck, having to squeeze through a gap between the seats that was a lot narrower than it had been earlier. There was no sound at all from up front, and Fred was suddenly afraid to speak, lest *something* answered. He followed the bobbing light from the flashlight out of the truck.

Sarah sat on her knees in the dirt beside the prone body of the scientist. The blood on Mullins' face looked black as tar in the flashlight. Her eyes had rolled up into their sockets, and her breath came in short, fast hitches.

"Doc, we *really* need you out here," Charlie shouted.

"We need some light," Doc's voice came from the dark in the back of the truck.

Charlie shone the beam back towards the truck to show Doc the way and the truck rocked and creaked as the three people in the rear started to pull themselves out.

Fred's eyes were starting to adjust to the darkness. The truck was little more than a black shadow, but it still had some power—the dashboard lights were on, shining bright in the gloom. While Doc got down out of the truck, Fred went to check on the two men up front.

The driver hadn't made it. He lay, slumped in his belt, neck obviously broken, his head hanging limply at too sharp an angle. If that hadn't killed him, the steering wheel embedded in his chest would have finished the job.

The man in the passenger seat was still alive, breathing heavily, but out cold. His face looked red in the dashboard lights.

*Like one of Big Bill's demons.*

He fought down an urge to flee, and opened the passenger door, having to tear it forcibly away from its hinges before he could reach the injured man. The guard moaned in response to the tearing of metal, but he didn't wake up. When Fred tried to get the guard out of the seat, he quickly found that the man was pinned in position by a mass of crushed metal and plastic below his waist. Fred smelled gasoline, oil—and blood.

"If you've got time, Doc," he said. "We've got a man in bad shape here too."

Fred lifted the automatic rifle from where it lay on the man's belly. He made sure he did it slowly and carefully.

*It wouldn't do to shoot the guy I'm trying to save.*

He put the gun on the ground, just as Doc spoke.

"Mullins needs me," she said. "How's your guy doing?"

"Trapped by the legs and losing blood, but I don't know how much."

"I'll give you a hand," the sheriff said, climbing down out of the truck.

But even between the two of them they couldn't

shift the mangled mass that was tangled around the trapped man's legs. The sheriff put his whole strength into it, and only managed to shift the wreckage an inch. Fred leaned across the wounded man, feeling hot breath on the back of his neck, as warm as a hair dryer.

"It's no use, Sheriff," he said. "He's held tight. We ain't getting him out of here anytime soon."

As Fred bent over him again to try a different angle of approach, the man's radio crackled, so loud that Fred jumped and banged his head on the roof.

"Find that radio," the sheriff said. "It might be our way out of here."

It took a few seconds to locate the small radio that was tucked deep inside the man's flak vest. As Fred got it out, it crackled again.

"Winton. This is home base. Come in."

Fred held the radio up, then realized he had no idea which button to press to reply. He handed it to the sheriff. The big man pressed a button and spoke.

"Sheriff Wozniak here. We need help, and we need it now."

To the credit of the man on the other end, he wasted no time asking futile questions.

"How many are you?"

"Six civilians, and three of your folks, one dead, two wounded and not ready to be moved. We're at the bottom of a hole in the Western Road, and I've no idea how deep we are."

"Sit tight. We're on our way."

* * *

The trapped man woke up a couple of minutes later and immediately moaned in pain.

"What happened?"

As if it came naturally to him, Charlie took charge of the situation. He handed the wounded man the bottle of JD.

"We crashed," he said, dryly. "And you're stuck until help gets here. I ain't got nothing for the pain but old Jack here, so I suggest you get it down you while you can."

"There's a field kit under my seat," the man said. "But I'll take my medicine any way I can get it."

While Charlie tried to get under the seat, the man drank from the mouth of the JD bottle, and the level of liquor inside had dropped markedly when he passed it to Fred.

"Don't give me any more unless you have to," the soldier said. His eyes were dark pits in a pale face, lit red by the dashboard lights. The sheriff passed the man the radio.

"They're on their way," he said. "Just hang tight."

Doc looked up from where she knelt by Mullins.

"They'll have to be quick," she said softly.

Fred looked down. Mullins was unconscious, her face a bloody mask.

"Her left lung's punctured, I think," Doc said, rising "And there may be other internal bleeding."

Charlie drew a squat case out from under the passenger seat.

"Anything here that will help?"

The case contained a field medical kit. Doc opened it and checked the contents.

"Not much that'll help the internal bleeding. The

best I can do is to make sure she's not in pain. There's enough morphine here to keep an elephant quiet."

"Morphine is always good," the wounded soldier in the passenger seat said. "I wouldn't mind some myself."

"Move aside," Doc said to Fred and the sheriff. "Let's see if there's at least someone here I *can* help."

Sarah was still on her knees by Mullins, head down and not speaking. Fred stepped away to stand beside the sheriff and Ellen Simmons, who, for once, seemed struck speechless by the situation. The only sound came from the intermittent tumble of fresh dirt down the walls of the hole.

Fred saw that the sheriff had the army man's rifle in his hands.

"It's more light we need," Fred said. "Not bullets."

The sheriff smiled, and flicked a switch on the gun. A powerful beam shone out from a top-mounted flashlight, just for a second or so before he switched it off.

"Best to save it until we *really* need it," the big man said.

The trapped man spoke.

"There's spare clips in my vest. Probably best if you have them too."

Doc helped the man shuck off the flak vest. Big Bill managed to put it on, a tight fit over his large frame.

"Anything else in the truck we can use?" the sheriff asked.

The trapped man tried to speak, coughed, and bubbled blood down his front. He wiped it away, and finally spoke.

"Nope. Sorry. All the good stuff is back at base camp. But don't worry. They'll get us out soon enough."

Doc turned away from the soldier. She looked worried.

"Did they say how long they'd be?"

The sheriff shook his head. Doc leaned over and whispered in the sheriff's ear. Fred didn't need to be a lip-reader to catch her gist.

*He's not going to make it.*

Ellen Simmons chose that moment to do something stupid again.

"Well, I'm not waiting here. We were nearly at the town limits. It can't be far."

She walked off into the gloom. Charlie shone the flashlight after her, lighting her up and throwing a huge shadow up the hill. The woman scrambled up the slope of stone and earth left by the collapse, each step bringing fresh falls of rock and rubble.

"Ellen," the sheriff shouted. "Get your ass back here. You're going to bring it all down around us."

The woman showed no signs of hearing him. Her scrambling got more frantic as it became obvious she was achieving little more than climbing in the same spot as more pebbles and dirt tumbled around her.

"I'll get her," Charlie said, when the sheriff moved to head in that direction. The older man walked over and started to clamber after the woman, the flashlight waving wildly as he climbed. Fred heard Charlie shout.

"You really are a stupid bitch, Ellen."

The only other sound was the rapidly growing

tumble and rush of dirt as the pair scrambled up the slope.

"Get back here," the sheriff shouted. "It's not safe."

The woman started to slide backward, sending more rock and dirt sliding.

"Grab her, Charlie," Fred shouted.

Charlie lunged for her.

He was too late. The slope gave way; Fred didn't know who had been the cause. The air suddenly filled with the roar of falling rock and the taste of dirt and dust. Somebody screamed. The beam of Charlie's light cut off abruptly, and they were left again in near darkness, only the dashboard lights providing a hellish red glow off to Fred's left.

He felt a hand take his, just as the sheriff switched on the rifle light.

"Everybody okay?" the sheriff asked.

Sarah squeezed Fred's hand.

"We're good here."

"Charlie?" Fred asked.

The sheriff shone the light towards the site of the latest rock fall. A new hole had formed just yards in front of their position. It fell away into blackness far below. There was no sign of either Charlie, or the Simmons woman. Fred and the sheriff walked over to the collapsed area. The sheriff shone the light down. Apart from rock walls and dirt, there was nothing to be seen.

"Charlie?" Fred shouted. His voice echoed back at him, and there was an answering *scrambling* from far below. He peered into the dark, hoping for a glimpse of light to show that Charlie was still there, still capable of using the flashlight. There was only more darkness.

"Charlie!" Fred shouted again. He may even have jumped down into the new hole had Big Bill not put a hand on his shoulder, just as another slide of rock and pebbles crashed down into the deep.

Silence fell.

"Charlie?" Fred said, barely able to manage more than a whisper.

"Ain't nobody coming back up out of there," the sheriff said softly.

Fred looked down again, and was forced to agree.

*Charlie's gone.*

Later, Fred might have time to process the fact, but for now he immediately found himself being thankful that the Simmons woman wouldn't be around to bitch and moan, then just as quickly was ashamed of himself for having the thought.

"What now, Bill?" he said.

The sheriff was still peering down the hole.

"We wait. Help is on its way."

*You sure of that, big man?*

Fred thought it, but didn't voice it.

A shuffle in the dirt behind them made them turn around. Doc stood there, the bottle of JD at her lips.

"Shouldn't you save that for your patients?" Sarah asked.

Doc took another swig, then passed the bottle to Fred.

"I've got no patients left. They're dead, both of them."

In less than a minute, their numbers had been halved, from eight to four.

Fred took the bottle from Doc, and wished they had several more like it.

# 21

Janet wished she'd held on to the JD bottle. Her mouth and throat tasted of dust and death, and she knew it would be a long time before she forgot the sight of life leaving the young soldier's eyes. Mullins had gone seconds after that without regaining consciousness. Janet had only just been able to see the woman's face in the red glow afforded by the dashboard lights, but that was enough. Her eyes, sunk back and black in the gloom, stared, unblinking at the ceiling before Janet bent over and gently closed them.

She felt helpless, her mind taking her back to a hospital internship where patients had died on her watch while she tried to save them. She felt the same sense of despair and frustration now as she had then.

*But at least back then I knew why; drunk drivers, crack addicts, just plain accidents. But here, now? I don't have a clue as to what or why.*

She couldn't see that situation changing anytime soon. She moved to stand beside Bill, and put an arm around the big man's waist, taking what comfort she could from the solid, steadfast man. Fred swigged from the JD, and passed the bottle around. Both Bill, and the girl, took a share, but Janet waved it away.

*If I really wanted oblivion, there's plenty of morphine left in the field kit.*

Bill still had the rifle light switched on. He panned it around, finally allowing them to see exactly where the truck had ended up.

They stood in a rough chamber, some thirty feet below the level of the road. Any chance they might have had of clambering out had gone in the most recent rock fall. Now it looked like the sides were nearly sheer, and still crumbling. On the far side of the truck were two darker patches in the shadow.

*Caves?*

The only sound was a rustle of fresh falls of dirt tumbling into the hole below them.

"How long, do you think?" Janet asked Bill.

"Ten minutes, tops, from when we talked," he said. "They'll be here any minute."

They stood, huddled close together, waiting for a sound or a light from above to tell them that help was at hand.

None came.

* * *

"I think we've got to assume they're not coming," Bill said twenty minutes later. He'd tried the radio three times in that period, and got nothing but static in reply. He put the radio away in a pocket of the flak jacket.

Janet felt panic rise up, and pushed it away.

*Now is not the time.*

"Can we climb?" she asked.

"I don't see how," Bill replied. "It'll crumble under our weight as soon as we try. There are no obvious handholds, and it's too steep anyway. I think our only chance is to go through there."

He washed a beam of light over the cave entrances they'd spotted earlier.

"But we don't know where they lead," she started, then realized that Bill knew that already. But he needed to be doing something, she could see that fact in his face, could feel it in the tension in his body.

"How about you two," the sheriff said, talking to Fred. "Ready to head out?"

Sarah looked up from Fred's shoulder and nodded.

"We ain't safe here," the girl said. "I can feel it."

Janet, although she would never voice it, felt exactly the same way. There was something oppressive about their situation, and she felt on edge, as if they were being watched, not by one person, but by a crowd, hiding just out of sight in the shadows. She thought of them as pale, thin, with big eyes.

"How about you, Fred?" Bill asked.

Fred nodded.

"What the lady says. It don't feel right just standing here. I've been spooked enough for one lifetime. I'd feel better on the move."

"Let's go then," Bill said, and started out.

"What about Mullins and the others?" Janet said.

Bill stroked her cheek with his free hand.

"Ain't nothing we can do for them right now," he said. "We'll come back for them."

There were three unspoken words at the end of that sentence, but Janet heard them in her mind as they moved out.

*If we can.*

* * *

Janet stood to one side of Bill, allowing him use both his hands and plenty of room to swing the rifle if need be. She tried not to look at the truck or the bodies as they passed, but when she bent to pick up the field kit, she felt the dead eyes of the soldier, accusing her. She stood quickly and followed Bill as they headed across the chamber.

One of the cave entrances was slightly bigger, but both were big enough to walk into.

"Which one?" Janet whispered.

"You got a light, Fred?" Bill asked. Fred passed him a lighter. The sheriff flicked it on and walked to the nearest cave mouth. The flame held steady and didn't flicker. He walked to the other entrance. The flame guttered and wafted in a breeze.

"Air's gotta come from somewhere," Bill said. He walked forward and shone the beam down the chosen passage. It looked to be mostly stone, and rough-hewn, possibly even man-made.

"Did the Hopman mines stretch this far?" Janet asked.

"Not that I know of," Bill replied. "But the old man was quite the one for digging where he shouldn't, so it wouldn't surprise me."

"What if we meet..." Janet's voice trailed off, but Bill knew what she meant.

"Ain't much we can do about that, except hope that this here light is strong enough to keep them at bay...unless you've got any other ideas?"

She shook her head.

"I just want to get up to the road as quick as we can."

"You and me both," Bill said.

The four of them went into the tunnel.

Janet was pleased to see that they were on a slight slope upward, and the feel of fresh air on her cheeks gave her more hope. But that was quickly quelled a few minutes later when they came to the first junction. Three dark tunnels faced them, and all three had enough of a draught coming through to cause the lighter to flicker when tested.

Bill shone the light along each tunnel in turn.

"Just more of the same," he said. "I'm of a mind to keep bearing west, which will be the one on the right if I still have my bearings."

"Whatever you say, Sheriff," Fred replied. "I'm a visitor here myself."

The girl at his side laughed at that, a sound so unexpected that Janet found herself joining in. The sound echoed around them, leaving behind whispers in the shadows before fading. Just as Bill stepped into the right-hand tunnel, an answering laugh echoed around them, one with no trace of humor in it, dull, like a recording of a recording.

"Behind, or in front?" Bill said, sweeping the whole area with light while turning in a circle.

"I couldn't tell," Janet replied.

"Behind. Definitely behind," Sarah replied. Her eyes were wide, and Janet saw white at her knuckles where she gripped Fred's hand.

Janet was suddenly struck by a terrible thought. "The bodies!"

She would have headed straight back to the accident site if Bill hadn't put a hand on her shoulder.

"They're dead," he said softly. "And we're alive. I want to stay that way. Come on. Double time."

Bill led them up the right-hand tunnel at a fast walk.

They met another junction in less than a hundred yards.

*It's a warren.*

Bill didn't hesitate, taking the rightmost exit. He set a fast pace, and Janet started to breathe heavily after only a few more minutes. Sarah was struggling to keep up, and Fred had to take much of her weight just to keep her moving.

"We need to slow," Janet said. "Just a bit."

"The draught's getting stronger," Bill replied. "I think we're nearly out."

* * *

They turned a corner, and the passageway opened up into a much wider chamber. Rubble—the tumbled remains of at least one house lay strewn across the space ahead of them. Bill waved the beam of light around the area. Once again they stood in the bottom of a deep hole, with sides too steep to even contemplate a climb. Stars showed in a patch of sky high above; the opening was thirty feet or so away, but it might as well have been thirty miles.

"This might take longer than I thought," Bill said. He washed light over the rubble. "See if there's anything salvageable; just stuff we can carry. I'll keep watch."

Janet joined Fred and Sarah in a scramble through the wreckage. Every time they shifted a larger piece of wood aside she held her breath, fearing they might expose a body underneath. But it seemed that the owners hadn't been home at the time of the collapse.

*Or maybe they were, and have already been taken?*

She immediately regretted ever having *that* thought, for all of a sudden she again felt as if there were watchers all around, lurking in the shadows. She tried to keep her mind on the task at hand.

"Got something," Fred said. He shifted a door aside, reached down, and came up with a packet of biscuits. Further rummaging produced some bottled water, peanuts and dried fruit. Sarah even found a shoulder bag that, once dusted off, served as a carrier for the food.

"At least we won't starve," Fred said dryly.

"If we're to be down here *that* long, I'm planning on going mad first," Janet replied, aware of just how close to the truth the remark might be.

Something shifted in the rubble just six feet from where Janet stood. She scuttled backward towards Bill. At the same time, Fred and Sarah backed away, leaving them on the far side of the wreckage from Janet and the sheriff. Wood creaked and moved, dust rose to float in the beam of light…and three too-tall, too-thin figures came up out of the ruined house.

"Weemean," the nearest one said, and raised a hand.

The sheriff wasn't taking any chances this time. He stepped forward, aiming the light straight at the lead figure. It started to waver and melt.

"Weemean," the voice said again, and was joined by others, the two figures behind it...and more, many more, from the dark shadows around them. Even in the gloom Janet was aware of grayer shapes in the darkness, coming closer.

"Bill?" she said.

"I see them," the big man replied. "Fred, get your ass over here. It looks like we're leaving."

Fred and the girl started to circle around the rubble. Pale shapes came out of the darkness behind them, arms reaching.

"Run!" Janet shouted.

Luckily the other pair didn't need to be told twice.

The sheriff chose a passageway and headed for it. All four of them reached it at the same time and together they fled into darkness lit only by the swinging beam from the flashlight on the rifle. A sound followed them, a high cry, almost mournful, from a choir of voices.

*Weemean.*

# 22

The sheriff led them at a flat run for several hundred yards in a tunnel that dipped slightly downward before bringing them to a halt at another junction.

"We're going the wrong way," Big Bill said. They were all breathing heavily and Fred had worked up a sweat that tricked down the back of his shirt.

"I ain't going back," Sarah said. "If that's what you're thinking."

She gripped Fred's hand and squeezed, tight.

"I'm with her," Fred said. "We need to keep going. It's got to lead *somewhere.*"

Doc was looking at the ground.

"Shine that light over here, Bill. We've got something."

The sheriff did as he was asked and shone the light on the floor of the tunnel. A parallel set of lines led off into the distance.

*Tracks. Like those of a cart?*

"I think we've found one of old man Hopman's tunnels," Doc said.

The sheriff agreed.

"And where there's tracks, there's a starting point...and maybe a way out."

"But it's going down," Sarah said. "Ain't we supposed to be going up?"

Before Big Bill could answer, sounds of padding footsteps echoed down the tunnel from behind them.

"Weemean," a chorus of voices shouted, the echoes in the confined space making it sound like there was a massed throng coming through the dark towards their position.

Big Bill didn't hesitate.

"Follow me," he said.

*It ain't like we've got much choice.*

Doc went in the middle behind Bill.

"You should go ahead a bit," Fred said to Sarah, "I'll watch our backs."

She laughed. "And what do you plan to do if there's anything there? Use harsh language?"

Fred managed a rueful grin. "You never know..."

Sarah kept a tight grip on his hand as they followed the sheriff's bobbing and swaying flashlight down the tracks. "I can swear real loud," she said, still smiling. "Just say when."

Fred hoped he wouldn't have to.

He looked over his shoulder every twenty seconds for a while, but there was only a blackness that his imagination was only too happy to fill with ghostly miners and grasping hands. He concentrated on putting one foot in front of the other and following Bill's lead as they went down ever deeper.

The air got steadily warmer, almost uncomfortably so, and Fred breathed in an acrid tang that immediately brought to mind Charlie's story of the dump sites he'd found in the shafts.

"Maybe this ain't such a good idea, Bill," he said.

The Sheriff slowed, wiping sweat from his brow. "I'm starting to think that myself," the big man replied. "Take a few seconds. I want to try the radio again."

"Ain't gonna get no signal down here, boss," Fred said, and then stopped when he saw the look on the Sheriff's face. The man needed to try something, anything.

Bill flicked on the handset.

"This is Sheriff Wozniak. If anyone can hear me, come back."

He pressed the receive button and they waited. There was nothing but the hiss of static. He was about to press it again when the static cleared and a voice Fred had never expected to hear again spoke.

"Is that you, boss?"

*Charlie?*

"Good to hear you, old man," the sheriff replied. Where are you?"

"Damned if I know. We fell into the hole; then the rest started coming down on top of us. We've been wandering around for a while, and I found another one of the feds' trucks. That's where we are now."

"Anybody else there with you?"

"Got Ellen here. She's banged up, but walking. There's some dead folks too."

"Anything you can use? Weapons?"

"I got a rifle and some light. And tell Doc we've got more morphine."

"Can you get up to safety?"

"Nope."

That one word spoke volumes. Fred knew Charlie well enough to hear the near despair in it, despite not being able to see the old man's face.

"Stay put. We're coming back up," Bill said.

"Back up? How far down have you got?"

"We found some cart tracks. Reckon we're in old Hopman's workings. It certainly smells like it."

"Then stay put," Charlie replied. "We passed an exit a couple of minutes ago where I caught a whiff of something I recognized. We're coming to you. Over and out."

* * *

They stood, huddled close, waiting for any noise of approach. The sheriff shone the flashlight back up the tunnel and Fred tried to breathe calmly, despite his whole body wanting to either run, or hide…or both. He expected at any instant for a horde of pale figures to advance out of the darkness.

"Fred is dead," a voice said, but whether it was close or far it was hard to tell in the narrow tunnel.

"I don't like this one bit, Big Bill," Fred said. "We can't stay here."

Sarah gripped his hand tighter as the sheriff replied.

"We'll give them a couple of minutes. We can't just leave them here."

*Why not? We did just that not too long ago.*

He immediately felt ashamed of himself for the thought. He dug in his pocket and brought out a crumpled cigarette packet, having to smooth a smoke out before lighting it and sucking in a lungful that immediately dispelled the acrid tang. That, and the fact they were not under immediate attack, managed to give him some kind of control, but he was far from calm, even before the voice came again.

"Weemean."

Shadows gathered just beyond the range of the sheriff's light.

"Charlie?" Big Bill shouted. "Is that you?"

"Fred is dead," a choir of voices replied.

A score of red demons walked forward, stopping at the farthest range of the light.

"Weemean."

It had come to resemble a chant, rising in a repeated chorus that echoed around them.

"Back," Bill said. "Head down the tunnel. I'm right behind you."

Fred tried to lead the way, but Bill had to keep the light on the advancing demons, and Fred was only able to see a few yards ahead. He was forced to walk slowly.

*Wouldn't do to go falling into any holes.*

Behind him, Bill cursed, and fired a short volley of bullets back up the tunnel, the sound almost deafening in the confined space.

"We need to go faster," Doc shouted.

"Then we need some light this way," Fred replied. "It ain't safe otherwise."

Bill fired another short burst back up the corridor, turned and sent a wash of light down the tunnel. It looked safe for at least twenty yards.

"Twenty paces," he said to Fred. "Then give me a shout, and we'll do it all again."

"Yes, boss," Fred said.

They repeated the twenty-pace routine five times, each time with Bill sending a volley of shots back up the tunnel before turning and lighting the way ahead. Fred, with Sarah still gripping tight to his hand, kept his eyes forward, peering into the gloom.

He felt warmer air on his face, just before the corridor took a sharp turn that opened out—a fact he only knew from the echoes that ran around them.

"Bill, I need some light."

By now all four of them had entered what proved to be another small chamber, one with two other exits. Bill also shone the light up above, but this wasn't a collapsed hole; a rock ceiling hung three feet overhead.

The demons' chant came down the tunnel they had just exited.

"Weemean."

It was answered from both the other exits, close and getting closer fast.

"Weemean."

"Get in a group," Bill shouted, and they moved to huddle together in the center of the chamber, just as the entrances of all three tunnels filled with the press of red demons.

"Weemean."

* * *

They all moved in rotation as Bill tried to maintain a travelling beam of light that would wash over all three entrances and keep the attack at bay. But there were too many of them; the demons came forward en masse, crowding into the chamber.

Sarah screamed; Bill fired a volley of shots, and the demons chant became almost deafening.

*"Weemean. Weemean."*

"We're going left," Bill shouted. "In three, two, one. Move!"

They all moved as one. Fred had to tug Sarah sharply towards him as two pairs of arms reached for her, and the shift of weight almost threw them both off their feet. Fred staggered, almost fell, and then was running just behind Bill and Doc, Sarah still gripping tight to his hand. The sound of the rifle boomed around them, along with an accompanying roar of defiance from both Bill and, joining him almost immediately, Doc.

The passageway directly ahead was filled with red bodies, melting away under the strength of the light and the force of the bullets.

More demons pressed behind the fallen.

Big Bill kept running, trying to reload the weapon as he did so. Sarah tripped again, and Fred had to drag her to her feet, and swing her away from more grasping hands. The demons were right behind them.

*We're not going to make it.*

Another burst of rifle fire sounded out, and Fred was confused at first, for Bill was still trying to reload.

"Close your eyes," a well-known voice shouted, and seconds later the chamber flared into blazing light. Fred saw yellow spots in front of his eyes, felt fresh heat on his face.

"Over here," the voice called. Charlie, with Ellen Simmons at his side, stood in one of the cave entrances, his feet covered in sloughing *gloop*. A rescue flare burned in the chamber just off to the left. "Come on," Charlie shouted. "It won't burn forever."

Fred led Sarah into the tunnel, feet splashing among what was left of the demons, half-blind from the aftereffects of the flare burst. Doc followed. Bill stopped beside Charlie.

"Good to see you again, old man," the sheriff said.

"You can thank me later," Charlie said. Outside in the cavern the flare fizzled and steamed, burning itself out. Shadows grew darker.

"Weemean," the chorus sounded from the passageways, deep and mournful.

"Time to go," Charlie replied. He took another flare from the pocket of a flak jacket, pulled the thread and tossed it just past the mouth of the tunnel where they stood. "Lead on, Bill."

"Where are we headed?"

"Down. As far down as we can go. It's the only way out that I know of."

They turned away as the second flare exploded in light. It threw flickering shadows ahead of them as they descended.

There was no time for questions. The sheriff led the way, with Doc at his side. Fred and Sarah, still hand in hand, followed, with Charlie and the Simmons woman bringing up the rear. Charlie barked out directions every time they came to a junction in an authoritative voice that brooked no argument.

They went down.

There was no further sign of the demons, but they heard them well enough, the chant, constant now, coming down the tunnel behind them.

*Weemean.*

"Shouldn't we be going up?" Sarah whispered.

Fred didn't answer. He was remembering an earlier conversation with Charlie, back before everything went to hell. Charlie had been talking about old man Hopman.

*He had some kind of operation going on down at the deepest level.*

"I think I know where Charlie's heading," he finally replied. "But I ain't too sure we're going to like what we find there."

# 23

Janet stayed close to Big Bill as they headed down. It was getting warmer, and drier. The air tasted like stale smoke, tickling at the back of her throat. The flickering beam of the rifle-mounted flashlight started to give her a tension headache behind her left eye. She looked down, concentrating on the ground underfoot, following the parallel tracks. They were clearer here, as if used more recently.

It seemed that Charlie was following the same route. Every direction he gave always had a set of tracks at their feet. Janet saw signs that they were in worked tunnels; shoring timbers, tool marks on the rock, and even a small pile of ancient cigarette butts against the wall. And it became even more obvious when they passed through a completely timbered section and walked past an overturned cart that was too rusted up to move.

"Nearly there," Charlie called out. "Just keep moving."

*Nearly where?*

The chanting behind them seemed farther away now, as if whatever had attacked them had given up the chase. Now that there was some distance from the event, Janet's thoughts turned from immediate survival to trying to rationalize what happened. But no matter how much she wanted it to make sense, a solution continued to elude her. Matters did not become any clearer when they arrived at the destination Charlie had been leading them to.

She knew they were there when Bill stopped suddenly, and swore loudly.

"Shit, Charlie. Where have you brought us?"

They looked out over a larger chamber. The far side was dominated by what looked like a recent collapse. What little light there was came up out of the hole, red and flickering, as if there were flames burning in the deep. Charlie and Ellen Simmons joined the other four at the tunnel mouth, looking out. The older man pointed to the left. There were two further tunnels there.

"The left one is a bunker, I think; old man Hopman's bolt hole. The right one leads to a storeroom, then up and out to daylight. That's the way we go."

"What was over there?" Fred Grant asked, pointing at the smoking hole.

"That was where the old man dumped all the chemical shit. We shouldn't go anywhere near it."

Janet almost laughed.

"I wasn't about to," she said.

Big Bill looked up the tunnel behind them.

"You take the lead this time, Charlie. You know where you're going. I'll watch our backs."

Janet hung back as the others moved out so that she could stay beside Bill.

Charlie led them around the wall of the cavern. He walked past the leftmost entrance without a glance. When Janet passed it, she glanced into the tunnel mouth. There was indeed a heavy iron door there, less than six feet away. It was closed, and despite her curiosity, she felt no immediate desire to see if it was locked. With Bill at her back she followed the others into the right-hand tunnel.

* * *

The walls flickered with dancing shadows on a shifting red background, like a disco in a nightmare. Charlie raised a clenched fist, and went still. The rest took their cue from the older man and stopped. The only sound was a distant crackle of flames.

Then they heard it, coming from straight ahead, the now-feared chant, coming from a multitude of voices.

"Weemean."

The chant got closer.

Charlie looked around.

"Fight or flight?" he asked. He held two flares in his spare hand, the rifle in the other. "This is all we've got."

"I can't go back the way we came," Ellen Simmons said, a note of pleading in her voice. "I just can't."

"And for once, I'm with Ellen," Janet said in reply. "We've got to keep going forward."

Charlie looked to Fred, who in turn looked to Sarah. The girl nodded.

"We girls need to stick together. Onward and upward."

Bill laughed.

"You heard the womenfolk, Charlie. Lead on."

Charlie threw Bill a salute.

"Just be ready to fall back if I say so," the older man replied. "This ain't the time for heroics, and I ain't in a hurry to see any more dead folks."

Without another word Charlie turned and started up the tunnel. Janet was surprised to see Ellen Simmons follow him, almost close enough to touch.

*Something has happened there.*

She wasn't given time to think about it. Charlie led them into another open chamber. This one was a storeroom, and one that had been in use up until recently. There were dozens of large barrels of water, stacked containers of gasoline, and boxes of canned and dried food.

"What is this shit?" Fred Grant asked in a whisper.

Charlie turned back.

"I told you. Old Man Hopman had a bunker down here. And it looks like the family kept it stocked over the years since then. I guess paranoia runs in the family."

*Or madness.*

She didn't say it, for just then the chant rose again, coming out of the only other exit from the storeroom. Heavy footsteps, many of them, came closer at a run.

"Weemean."

"Here we go," Charlie said. "Get ready to run."

He stepped forward and flooded the tunnel ahead with light. As the first demon appeared he gripped the string on one of the flares, but didn't pull it. More demons joined the first, then more still until a mass of them started to flood from the tunnel mouth.

"For God's sake, Charlie!" Ellen Simmons shouted. The old man grinned, blew her a kiss, and pulled the string, in the same movement lobbing the flare into the approaching creatures.

Janet remembered to look away and close her eyes. She still got a bright yellow flash against her eyelids and a blast of heat on her face. There were no screams; no sound from the attackers. But when Janet opened her eyes, there was only an expanding puddle of *gloop* on the floor.

"Run!" Charlie shouted, and headed for the tunnel. The others didn't need a second telling. They followed the old man, splashing though the remains underfoot.

They didn't get far. The tunnel took a sharp turn ten yards in, but even before they reached the turning they heard the chant coming down from above them, and more heavy footsteps on the rock. Charlie strode forward, pulled the string on the last flare and lobbed it round the corner. He turned back almost immediately.

"There's no way out that way. Back the way we came. It's our only hope."

They retreated back as far as the cavern with the smoking pit, only to find that way too was blocked, as more demons streamed out to the tunnel they needed to take.

Charlie immediately moved to the only option

available to them; the entrance leading to the iron door.

"What if it's locked?" Ellen Simmons said.

'Then we fight," Charlie said grimly.

"Whatever you're going to do, make it fast," Bill said, as the six of them crammed into the space in front of the large door. Bill kept his weapon trained on the opening. The chant from beyond got louder again.

"Weemean."

Charlie turned the handle on the door. Iron creaked and complained, and for a long second Janet thought it wasn't going to open; then Charlie put his shoulder into it and the door swung open. They all but fell inside, slamming the door shut behind them just as the first of the demons slammed against it from the outside.

"Light. We need light," Janet shouted.

Bill obliged by lighting up the door. A demon showed its face in the portal window and just as quickly dropped away as the beam hit it.

"Got it," Charlie shouted. There was the sound of a switch being flicked, and suddenly everything got so bright that Janet's eyes took seconds to adjust. When they did, she got her first look at Hopman's *bunker.*

* * *

When Charlie had mentioned a bunker, Janet's first thought was of a concrete subterranean dwelling, like a nuclear shelter, with maybe some retro-styled fittings from the Cold War era, but at least with some creature comforts.

What was in front of her was far from modern. It was little more than a modified cave, lit by neon tubes overhead. There were several alcoves; one with a camp bed, one with a basic stove and sink arrangement, and one with a writing desk and bookcase. But the floor space was totally dominated by the carving etched directly into the rock. She had to stand back to get a sense of what she was seeing, and her heart sank as she understood.

*More of Bill's demonic shit.*

It was a pentagram, straight out of a Hollywood fantasy of satanic ritual, a five-pointed star with two external circles carved in a Cyrillic script Janet couldn't read. Skulls, all too human, sat at each point of the star, and thick wax candles sat in the valleys between the points. The whole diagram was some ten feet across.

"What the hell is this?" Bill said.

"*Hell* is the right word," Charlie replied, and spat on the floor. "Looks like old man Hopman found what he was looking for. I guess we know where he got his money."

Janet looked over at the older man.

"You're serious?"

Charlie didn't smile back.

"After what we've seen these past few days? Are you not?"

*He's got a point.*

"First things first," Charlie said. "We've got light, for now. Let's see what else Hopman has squirreled away down here."

Over the next five minutes they found that they

wouldn't starve; Hopman, the younger, had kept a well-stocked larder behind the stove, mainly canned and dried foods and a large supply of coffee. Ellen Simmons surprised them by taking charge of the stove.

"The menfolk need to be fed," she said, and smiled, straight at Charlie.

*Something definitely happened there.*

Fred Grant and the girl had already appropriated the camp bed, sitting side by side and sharing a cigarette. Bill and Charlie were off in the farthest corner of the cave, checking out the generator and ensuring the area was secure, leaving Janet feeling like the fifth wheel on the cart.

She headed for the writing desk, more in curiosity than any search for information. An old habit led her straight to a perusal of the books on the shelves at the back of the alcove. The titles meant nothing to her—*The Mysteries of the Wurm, The Twelve Concordances of the Red Serpent, The Sigsand mss* and many others; esoteric tomes from a bygone age that should have stayed gone.

The writing desk itself was a handsome piece of furniture of some vintage, the sort of thing Janet might wish to have in her own home, had it not been so obviously infested with mildew and rot. There were only two things under the roll-top lid—a ballpoint pen, and a thick leather-bound journal, filled with scrawled writing in several distinct hands. She started reading a passage near the middle of the book.

*"Still no joy. I've had them digging twenty-four hours a day. I know it's there. The Cree said it was, and I've felt the power for myself. Last night I performed the Saa-*

*mara Ritual in the barn out back. The Old One came to me again, asking for release. He promises much, but that will all be for nothing if I do not find the Gateway. It is there. It must be there."*

It was dated: August 23, 1973.

She skipped to the last entry, a crabbed, hard-to-read paragraph in a tight-spaced hand.

*"I can't control it. God help me. God help all of us. It's free. After all this time, it's free again."*

It was dated two days ago, and signed, Tom Hopman.

# 24

Fred looked up as Charlie and Bill returned from the rear of the chamber.

"Anything happening outside?" Bill asked, and Fred realized that nobody had even bothered to check while the two men were away. He stood, with Sarah as ever moving like a part of him at his side. He looked out of the small window. The glass was thick, obscuring some of the view, making it blurred and unclear. But he saw enough to know they weren't leaving anytime soon. The pit glowed red and orange. Around its rim, tall figures danced. They were mostly just dark shapes framed against the fiery glow behind them, but they were defined clearly enough that horns, tails and even talons were clearly visible.

*First ghosts, then bears, now fucking demons?*

Fred turned away, looked to Charlie, and shook his head. He didn't speak. He didn't need to. The older man nodded in reply.

"So, we wait," Charlie said. "Ain't not much else we can do."

Fred saw Ellen Simmons flinch at that, and expected a retort. But none came. The woman left the stove and went round the room serving coffee.

"There'll be corned-beef hash along in ten minutes or so," she said. "It ain't going to be much, but it'll be hot."

"Ellen, darling," Charlie said with a smile, waving towards the iron door. "It's as hot as hell in here already."

The woman actually blushed as she returned to the stove. Big Bill joined Doc over in the alcove with the writing desk, and Charlie sat down beside Fred and Sarah.

"You got any smokes left, lad?" the older man asked. "I'm pegged out."

"I'll swap you," Fred replied. "For a story. What happened after the rockslide? And don't try to dodge it. I can see the way she looks at you now."

Charlie looked grim.

"It ain't anything that should be told here," he said. "It should wait until we're back up in daylight, with the sun on our faces and beer in our hands. But if it'll pass the time..."

He took a cigarette from Fred, lit up, and started to speak, gazing off into a far distance, remembering.

* * *

"We didn't fall too far," he started, but we went sideways as well as down and when we came to rest, we had only rock above us and a wall of dirt at our backs we couldn't dig through. Ellen was in a bit of a state. She didn't even calm when I let her hold the flashlight. She was screaming fit to burst and I thought she'd bring more of those…things…down on us. So I shut her up."

"You *hit* her?" Sarah said. The shock was clear in her voice.

Ellen Simmons laughed and turned back from where she was working at the stove.

"No, dear. He kissed me. And right properly at that. I'm staying kissed."

Charlie looked sheepish.

"I didn't have any other choice. It worked though. She got quiet right quick."

He took a long drag from the cigarette, smiling to himself. Fred gave him a nudge.

"Okay, enough about your love life. How did you get out of there?"

"I'm an old hand in tunnels," Charlie replied. "You know that. I kept going right and up, where we could, hoping to find a way to the surface. I was half expecting to find the same tracks you found. Instead, we found more death."

He went quiet again, and when he spoke, it was in a whisper.

"Ain't gonna be much of a rescue for us," he said. "At least not for a while. We found what was left of the CDC folks in a new hole—a big hole. There were trucks and trailers piled over and into each other. And bodies. A lot of bodies."

A thought suddenly struck Fred.

'The injured? The ones that were with us last night?"

Charlie nodded, and a single tear ran from his left eye. He wiped it away angrily.

"Them too," was all he said in reply before continuing.

"Ellen was a rock. She helped me search the wreckage. Ain't no survivors. And there's worse. Some of the bodies looked melted, as if something had been at them, eating them."

Fred was remembering the burn Doc had taken outside the bar as Charlie went on.

"Anyway, to cut a long story short, I found the gun, the flares...and a radio. I hoped to get somebody up top, somebody to rescue us."

"And you got us instead," Fred finished. "Your run of good luck is holding."

Charlie sucked the last smoke from the cigarette and ground it out underfoot.

"We can't stay here," he said. "Not for too long. If I know the military mind, they'll be bombing the shit out of the town before too long. For all I know the order's already given."

"Surely that's a good thing?" Sarah asked. "They'll kill them all...all the bears."

"You ain't thought it through, girl. We're sitting on the edge of the source of the problem. Where do you think them bombs will target?"

"And there's something else we need to think about," Doc said. She walked across the floor, skirting the edge of the pentagram, deliberately not stepping on the lines. She carried a battered leather journal.

"You need to hear this."

* * *

"Food first," Ellen Simmons said. "Ain't no sense making decisions on an empty stomach."

"I'm not sure I want to eat, after what I just read," Doc whispered, but they all took a bowl of hash when offered, and there was silence as they ate.

"So, what's so important, Doc?" Charlie asked as he put his bowl down. "I take it you've found something that explains the mumbo-jumbo?"

It was Big Bill who replied.

"Mumbo-jumbo is right. If I'd known what Hopman was up to, I'd have thrown him in jail years ago."

"Charged with what?" Fred asked, pointing at the pentagram. "Being deluded ain't a crime."

"No," Bill replied. "But murder is. And Charlie... you ain't gonna like this. At least one of them skulls belongs to a man you knew."

*Fredisdead.*

It came as a whisper, from some corner of the cave they couldn't identify, and it wasn't repeated, but all six of them were on edge as Doc started.

* * *

"This is a record," she said, holding up the journal. "A record of a family obsession that goes back nearly a hundred and fifty years."

"Them grooves in the floor are older than that," Charlie replied. "I know my rocks."

"I'll get to that," Doc said. "But first, there's this."

She read from the start of the journal.

*"Two hundred dollars the land cost me; everything I*

*had and then some. But it will be worth it if the Old One is there, where the Cree say he is buried. Riches and power beyond the ken of man – that's what they say he promises. We'll see. But first, I need to find the Gateway. Myth and legend is all I have to go on. But if it's there, I'll find it."*

Doc looked up.

"It goes on in that vein for a long time. That first entry is dated in the 1870s, and signed, George Hopman, who I think must be the great-grandfather. And twenty years later, he was still searching. He'd started digging by then; the first of what would be many mineshafts. There's a lot of frustration in his writings. Until we get to the nineties. That's when things start to get *really* strange."

*"He has started to whisper to me, in the shadows, in the dark. He asks for rituals, for obedience, for sacrifice. And he is getting stronger. I have sent to Boston for advice. Maybe the Brethren can help."*

"The Brethren?" Fred said, interrupting. "What's that all about?"

Doc shrugged.

"I don't know. I'm guessing at some kind of esoteric secret society…the late part of the nineteenth century was rife with them. But that's not the important thing. Listen."

*"I still cannot find the Gateway, and fear I will be too infirm, and too short of sufficient funding, to complete the task. I leave this journal in the hands of my sons, to do with what they will, in the hope that they will complete the task and raise this family back up to where it once was."*

Doc looked up again.

"There's a twenty-year gap. In the early twenties, it's taken up again, in a different hand, signed James

Hopman. I believe he might be the father of the one Charlie calls *Old* Hopman. And it's with him that the *mumbo-jumbo* starts in earnest.

"The book is full of what I would have called nonsense before now; magical symbols, details of rituals performed and discarded as not working, recipes for potions and instructions for binding demons; the sort of thing I thought we'd left behind in the Dark Ages. And once again, the writer's tone is one of frustration, over the course of many years. This is from the forties."

Just as she bent her head to read again, Fred heard a whisper, from the alcove above the stove.

*We are with Fred. Fred is dead.*

None of the others showed any signs of hearing it, and once again it was not repeated, but he now only had half his attention on what Doc was saying, and he kept his gaze on the shadowy corners, ready to move at the merest hint of attack.

*"Twenty years we've dug. He's stronger than ever, and it takes the Saamara Ritual to keep him out of my head. But I ain't been able to get him to do my bidding. Sacrifice is what he demands, and I've given him chickens, pigs, even cattle. But it ain't enough. He wants more… more than I am prepared to give him. He says it will all be different when we find the Gateway."*

Doc stopped.

"His father might have quailed at the *demands*. But *Old* Hopman wasn't so squeamish. You might want to prepare yourself, Charlie. This will be rough on you. We arrive in the early seventies, and *Old* Hopman takes up the writing."

*"They found it last night. Fred made the breakthrough*

*into the chamber, so it was only fitting that he was the first to be given enlightenment. Who knew a man had so much blood in him? The Old One was pleased though, and hungry. He took the other two, and then together we hid the way so that the morning shift would not find it. It's mine now, and mine alone. He says it will not be long until he is strong enough to lift himself up, and that I will have to feed him. But I ain't stupid. The Samaara Ritual keeps him down, and any food he gets will only be whatever I chose to dump down there. I aim to thrive, and I can only do that by using what he gives me, and keeping him in the pit. I ain't about to go down in history as the man who brought hell on earth."*

Doc stopped.

"I think I know now what is going on here."

"Auld Nick. That's what's going on here," Bill said. "Demons and devils and bloody murder."

"I'm not so sure," Doc said. "Remember, I saw aliens, and Charlie saw VC. I *think* the Hopmans only saw demons and the devil because that's what they wanted to see. And because they've been *communicating* with the thing for so long, it has become...*imprinted*, for want of a better word, with the pattern of their thoughts and desires."

"Thing?" Charlie asked. "What kind of thing do you have in mind, Doc? I don't remember seeing anything like this on the National Geographic channel. Do you?"

Doc smiled grimly.

"I believe it's something new to science. Maybe something new in terms of the geological timeline. It's an organism, of a kind, but it'll take better minds than mine to fathom its secrets."

"That's all very well, Doc," Fred said. "But what do we do about it? How do we get out of here?"

"I may have an idea about that," Doc replied. At that precise instant, a voice spoke from the shadows.

*Weemean.*

* * *

Three figures stood in an alcove, wavering and flowing, the only steady facet of them being the red, staring eyes.

Charlie moved immediately; one second he was sitting next to Fred, the next he was on his feet, weapon pointed at the alcove, washing bands of light into the shadows. The demons melted back into the darkness.

"If you've got a plan, Doc, I suggest we get to it," he said. "I'm getting proper squirrelly down here."

Doc frowned.

"Loath as I am to say it, I think we should attempt a ritual."

Big Bill was first to reply.

"I ain't about to get involved in any of that satanic stuff, Janet. No way, no how. We'd be putting our souls at risk."

"Then we die here," Doc said quietly. "I don't see another way."

"We make a run for it," Sarah replied. "We've got the guns and the light...and there's all that gasoline outside. Surely we could do something with that?"

Charlie, who had started to pace the floor, went still, thinking.

*Weemean.*

This time the chant came from all around. Shadows crept in all the corners, danced in the alcoves. A dozen pairs of red eyes stared out of the dark.

"Get into the pentagram," Doc shouted. "It's our only hope."

Charlie had other ideas. He grabbed Ellen Simmons' hand and headed for the iron door. Fred looked at the diagram on the floor, and the shifting red figures that even now crept closer from the shadows. Doc had already stepped into the circle, and Fred saw that the sheriff was loath to leave.

"Come on, Bill. Charlie's got a plan."

The sheriff stood, halfway between the door and the pentagram, indecision freezing him to the spot. Fred was equally torn, between Bill, and Charlie, both of whom were the only two real friends he had in the world.

Sarah settled the matter for him. She tugged at his hand, dragging him towards the door.

"I ain't staying here to be ate by no bears," she said.

Fred gave in.

"Come with us," he said as they passed the sheriff.

But Big Bill was still in the same spot as Fred and Sarah ran through the door. Fred hit it hard in passing and it swung shut behind him with a clang that sounded like a death knell.

# 25

"Bill, come here," Janet said. "Into the protection."

She stood in the circle, frantically trying to find a page in the journal. She'd seen it earlier, but had failed to note its position relative to other passages.

*And now, when I need it, I can't find it.*

She sensed movement, looked up. Red eyes stared back at her from the alcoves and shadows. The neon light above flickered and dimmed, just slightly, but more than enough to allow the demons to creep farther into the chamber.

"Bill!" she shouted, more insistent this time. That got the sheriff moving, but still he refused to step into the circle, choosing instead to walk the perimeter, washing light into the dark places. It was obvious to Janet that he wouldn't be able to do enough to keep the things at bay for long.

"Sheriff," she shouted again. "Get your ass in here. I need you if we're going to help the others escape."

The appeal straight to his duty worked. Bill waved the light into the corners one final time, then stepped over the grooved outer circle to join Janet inside the pentagram.

The demons crowded forward into the chamber, flowing and melting in the light, but the sheer bulk of them were pressing more and more of their viscous material through. Very quickly, the etched circle was surrounded.

Their path to the iron door, their route of escape, was completely blocked.

*We have no way out.*

# 26

Fred led Sarah away from the tunnel mouth. Charlie was already there, washing beams of light across a small army of demons that danced and capered around the edge of the fiery pit. He was doing enough to keep them at bay, for now.

"Fetch the gas," Charlie shouted. "As much as you can get, as quick as you can get it."

Fred headed up the tunnel to where the gas was stored. There was just enough light to see the stacked containers.

Sarah still stood at his side.

"You'll have to let go of me, darlin'," he said. "Just for a bit. But I promise, I ain't going nowhere without you."

The girl let go, moved away...and started lugging a gas canister, having to half carry, half drag it across the floor. Normally Fred would have helped her out. But Charlie had been insistent.

"Get a move on, lad," the older man shouted from out in the main cavern. "I ain't gonna be able to hold them for long."

Fred looked up the tunnel; the one that they would have to use to escape. The walls showed signs of scorching where the flare had burned and raged, but there were no shifting shadows and no demons.

*Not yet.*

Fred lifted and carried in three separate short journeys with Sarah at his side. When they got back from the third trip, it was to find Ellen Simmons pouring the gas on the rock at her feet. The liquid slid downhill in a short stream that made a large puddle at the feet of the dancing demons and was already on the verge of overflowing and tumbling into the pit.

"Fire in the hole," Charlie shouted, and flicked his lighter alit.

Just as he threw it into the stream of gas, they heard high chanting rise from inside the bunker, coming clear even through the iron door.

# 27

Janet found the ritual in the journal just as the growing pool of *gloop* on the floor crept within inches of the outer protective circle. She stuttered over the first words, but found a rhythm that seemed apt, and almost sang out the unfamiliar sounds.

*"Ri linn dioladh na beatha, Ri linn bruchdadh na fal-luis, Ri linn iobar na creadha, Ri linn dortadh na fala."*

It was as if they stood inside a giant bell. The chamber rang and resonated, echoing the ritual back at her, amplifying and enhancing it until a whole chorus of voices joined in the chanting. Bill surprised her by lending his own voice to the effort. He moved beside her and put an arm around her waist as they chanted.

The *gloop* retreated away from the edges of the circle.

*This might actually work.*

# 28

The flame ran across the cavern floor and the nearest group of demons went up in a *whoosh* of heat and light and screaming. Fred felt a burst of burning air in his face, and smelled burnt hair at the same time as he felt his eyebrows curl. He turned his face away as the flash threatened to blind him, and when he looked back, there was no sign of any demons around the crater. Gray smoke rose from burning tissue; all that was left of the things that had stood there seconds earlier.

The chanting from the bunker rose to a new level of volume, so much so that it seemed to echo around them. An answering call came up out of the pit, piteous and wailing.

*Weemean.*

Charlie kicked over the remaining canisters, sending a flood of fire down over the edge.

The response was instantaneous. The walls shook,

dislodging stones and pebbles in a rain around them. A rock struck Fred just above the brow and he felt warm blood run past his ear.

"Time to go," Charlie said, and headed for the exit. Ellen Simmons followed him without question.

"What about Doc and Big Bill?" Fred said, starting to move for the iron door to the bunker.

Sarah pulled him away.

"She's buying us time. That's all she was ever going to do. And she knows it."

He didn't get close enough to see inside the bunker, but he heard two voices raised in unison. He felt the chant ring in his mind. It stayed with him as they fled.

*"Ri linn dioladh na beatha, Ri linn bruchdadh na falluis, Ri linn iobar na creadha, Ri linn dortadh na fala."*

# 29

*"Ri linn dioladh na beatha, Ri linn bruchdadh na falluis, Ri linn iobar na creadha, Ri linn dortadh na fala."*

The neon lights failed all at once, exploding in a burst of fragments that fell around Janet and Bill and causing the chant to falter and come to a halt.

Silence descended in the chamber. Darkness crept in the corners, and red eyes stared out at them.

Bill washed light from the gun where he could, but as soon as he passed a dark area, the shadows firmed again and demons came forward. He stepped away from Janet, obviously intent on getting closer to the alcoves. She tugged at his shirt.

"Stay in the circle," Janet said. "We need to start the chant again."

"We need to get out of here. Right now," the sheriff replied, and sent a volley of shots towards the bookcase alcove where the shadows were thickest.

"No," Janet said softly. "The chant is the only thing stopping it. If we leave now, it wins. We need to buy the others time to escape."

She started to chant again, feeling her throat tear, but putting everything into it, almost a scream this time.

*"Ri linn dioladh na beatha, Ri linn bruchdadh na fal-luis, Ri linn iobar na creadha, Ri linn dortadh na fala."*

Bill looked her in the eye.

"Janet. We need to go."

He put out a hand. She took it, and pulled him close. She couldn't stop the chant; she knew to do so would be the end of them all. Bill pulled against her, but not for long. She saw it in his eyes first before she felt his body relax.

*He's staying.*

The sheriff joined his voice to hers and once again the chamber rang with a chorus of chanting. Demons crowded all around the circle, red eyes flaring.

But none would cross the lines in the rock.

The encroaching figures moaned.

*Weemean.*

The floor underfoot shook, threatening to throw them off balance. Dust, then pebbles fell from the roof as the tremors increased. Janet kept chanting.

*"Ri linn dioladh na beatha, Ri linn bruchdadh na fal-luis, Ri linn iobar na creadha, Ri linn dortadh na fala."*

# 30

Fred and Sarah ran, hand in hand, just behind Charlie and Ellen Simmons. They met no resistance in the form of demons, but had more than enough to cope with from falling debris, shifting footing and a blast of noise from below that threatened to deafen them.

*Weemean. Weemean.*

It was only good luck and Charlie's foreknowledge that brought them up and out into tunnels that were in better shape, better able to cope with what seemed to be an imminent collapse.

A new tremor hit, a big one, causing Sarah to stumble and fall against him. As he helped her up, she looked him in the eye, then kissed him, hard, on the lips.

"You're stuck with me now, you know that, right?"

Fred kissed her back.

"I wouldn't have it any other way, darling. Let's get out of here and get our lives started."

They fled upward, into the light. Behind them the whole mine system began to collapse in on itself. They turned a final corner and emerged into watery morning sun, just as the tunnel fell in behind them with a soft *crump* and a puff of dust.

# 31

*"Ri linn dioladh na beatha, Ri linn bruchdadh na fallluis, Ri linn iobar na creadha, Ri linn dortadh na fala."*

Janet's voice faltered, her throat unable to take any more wounding, but Bill made up for it, bellowing out the chant at the top of his voice.

*It feels like we're in church. And in a way, maybe we are.*

More rock fell from the roof. The iron door collapsed off its hinges as the rock supporting it fell away, and a sudden slip of rock left their position in the circle open, giving them a clear view to the pit outside. Where before the pit had been filled with smoke and flame, now it was a rolling mass of tissue; the same material Janet was coming to know so well. It swayed and swelled, like a heavy sea. A dome formed in the center, rising up and taking shape, a tall figure, ten, twelve, sixteen feet tall, red wings sprouting from the back and unfolding until the wingtips touched the shaking walls on either side of the pit. Eyes the size of plates stared at them.

*Weemean.*

Janet had one last look at the journal, making sure she remembered the final phrase, the last act of the binding ritual.

"I love you," she said to Bill. Then, with the last of her voice, called out, *"Dhumna Ort!"*

The last thing she saw was the demon collapse in on itself. Bill pulled her close as the roof fell in on them, and everything went away.

# 32

A chopper spotted them on the side of a collapse some twenty minutes later, and ten minutes after that they were in the air. Sarah leaned against Fred, her head on his shoulder. He patted her hair, but most of his attention was on the view out of the window.

At first he wasn't sure what he was looking at; it took him several seconds to get his bearings. Then he saw the church, or rather what was left of it. It was now little more than a pile of rubble in the middle of what looked like a heavily ploughed field. Around it lay the remains of the town, now reduced to a series of fresh holes and collapsed houses. He was going to remark on it, but turned to see Charlie and Ellen in each other's arms in a warm embrace.

Fred turned back to the window, and allowed himself a small smile before remembering what had been lost, and especially the companions they had so recently left in the mine.

*Is it over? Is it really over?*

The chopper brought them down on the edge of a makeshift hospital some way to the east of town. They were headed for the tents when they heard the distant rumble as bombs went off.

"Sounds like the army boys finally got their fingers out their asses," Charlie said.

A tall plume of dust and smoke rose over the horizon. The ground underfoot trembled and shook, and Fred found that he was holding his breath, waiting for the vibration, the *hum* that would signal a fresh collapse. His heart raced, and all he wanted to do was run. Sarah gripped his hand, tight enough to bring pain.

The rumble receded, and the plume of smoke dispersed in the wind.

* * *

They spent several hours in the makeshift hospital as doctors and scientists prodded and poked and took more samples.

At one point Charlie looked over at Fred and winked.

"Looks like we both got lucky," he said, pulling Ellen close to him and kissing her full on the lips. Fred could do little else but laugh.

"Yeah. But what I really need is a beer."

He knew as he said it that he didn't really mean it. What he needed was right next to him. He pulled Sarah close, and she snuggled against him. Suddenly beer was the farthest thing from his mind.

"What say we blow this place and find a bar?"

Ellen said, and that got a laugh from all four of them.

Fred was feeling almost mellow, but the mood didn't last. A uniformed officer came into the tent and walked purposefully towards them.

"Come with me," he said, without a word of explanation.

"What if we don't want to?" Ellen replied, showing the first sign in a while of the woman she had been *before*.

The man's only reply was to put his hand on his pistol.

Charlie sighed.

"Looks like the beer will have to wait. Let's see what's in store for us now, shall we?"

They followed the army man out. A jeep waited outside the tent, and the officer motioned that they should get in.

"The general needs your opinion on something," he said as they climbed into the seats. Then nobody spoke as they drove off through what was left of the town, taking detours around holes and collapsed buildings. The scale of what had happened shocked them all into silence for the whole length of the journey.

When the jeep stopped, Fred realized he was home; or as close to it as he was likely to get. He got out of the jeep and stood amid the ruin of the trailer park. They had come to a halt at the edge of a deep hole.

*Is it the same one?*

He didn't want to get any closer, not knowing what he'd do if he looked down...and saw a mop of blonde hair down there in the dark. Wind whispered in his ears.

*Weemean.*

He almost jumped, but the others showed no signs of having heard anything.

"This is what the general wanted you to see," the army man said, and motioned them over to peer down into the hole.

Fred followed the others reluctantly to the edge and looked over.

There was a forest of pods lining the walls, going down into the dark as far as they could see. Each pod was long and elongated, almost like a head of corn. And inside each a figure, barely formed, writhed and twisted, all of them eager to be born.

Fred turned away, trying not to vomit.

"Why don't you just bomb the shit out of them too?" Charlie asked.

"The general needs to know," the army man said, his voice soft. "Are these the townsfolk? The missing people?"

Charlie spat at the man's feet.

"Do they *look* like people to you? You tell your general to get on with his *slash and burn*...and to do it right quick, before this spreads as far as County."

It was only then that Fred noticed the worry lining the officer's face.

"County have got enough problems," he whispered. "Seems like everybody in the state is coming down with headaches and nosebleeds."

* * *

The officer drove them back to the edge of town. No one spoke until they were once again outside the tents of the makeshift hospital. The soft *crump* of explosions sounded, and more smoke rose over the town.

Fred looked to Charlie. The older man appeared deep in thought.

"It *is* over, isn't it?" Ellen Simmons asked.

Charlie spat on the ground.

"Maybe; and maybe not. But I've been thinking about what Doc said about sacrifices. And nobody knows just how far the old tunnels spread below here. We can only hope the army know what they're doing. But I'll tell you something..."

He looked at Fred and winked.

"Ain't no way in hell I'm cleaning *this* mess up."

* * *

Together, the four of them walked out of the disaster zone.

As they approached an armed barricade, one of the guards sneezed into a handkerchief, soaking it with fresh blood.

Fred tensed, but no one stopped them as they passed through.

They walked on. Neither he nor the others looked back.

# ABOUT THE AUTHOR

William Meikle is a Scottish writer, now living in Canada, with fifteen novels published in the genre press and over 250 short story credits in thirteen countries. His work has appeared in a number of professional anthologies and magazines. He lives in Newfoundland with whales, bald eagles and icebergs for company.

ained at www.ICGtesting.com

/480/P

9 781937 771973

CPSIA information can be ob
Printed in the USA
BVOW09s0413051214
377659BV00023B